BETTER THAN HEX

SPELLBOUND PARANORMAL COZY MYSTERY, BOOK 5

ANNABEL CHASE

RED PALM PRESS LLC

Better Than Hex

A Spellbound Paranormal Cozy Mystery, Book 5

By Annabel Chase

Sign up for my newsletter here http://eepurl.com/ctYNzf and or like me on Facebook so you can find out about new releases.

Cover Design by Alchemy

❀ Created with Vellum

CHAPTER 1

THE SKY WAS A BRILLIANT BLUE, as though the clouds had parted in honor of my special day. This afternoon I was to receive a ceremonial key to the town for my role in reversing a youth spell on the Spellbound town council and apprehending the responsible party—a nasty wizard called Felix.

I rifled through my closet, unsure what to wear. The ceremony was to take place on the grounds of the Mayor's Mansion so I needed something suitable for outdoors. Which outfit said humble yet thrilled? The thought of being in the spotlight was unnerving. I didn't mind attention in the Great Hall, where I defended my clients. It was different when the sole purpose of the event was to put me on display, though. Not that I didn't appreciate the award. The only other award I'd ever received in my life was the penmanship award in fifth grade. My penmanship wasn't even particularly neat, but, because I was left-handed, it seemed that Mrs. Roberts felt I had overcome a significant handicap. Apparently most left-handed children she'd taught had the handwriting of a distressed chicken.

I pulled a dress from the closet and held it against me, scrutinizing my reflection in the mirror.

"Do you really think that's the right outfit for the occasion?" Gareth asked, ever the skeptic.

I glared at my vampire ghost roommate. "What's wrong with this dress? It says responsible yet feminine."

He folded his arms. "It says boring yet oddly high maintenance."

"It does not," I countered. "And I am the least high maintenance person I know. My maintenance is low. Very low."

Gareth rolled his eyes. "If you say so."

I returned the dress to the closet and chose a different one. "Hey, I'm not the one who alphabetized cans in the pantry."

"It just made things easier," he insisted. "It's a mess in there now. You've destroyed a life's work in a matter of months."

"Well, if you ever manage to move physical objects again, the pantry can be your first port of call." As a ghost, Gareth was unable to manipulate objects in the physical world. I'd hired him a tutor in the form of Lyra Grey, one of the notorious Grey sisters. She'd been working with Gareth to improve his skills in the ghost department.

"I've been making excellent progress and you know it," he said.

I held up the next dress for inspection. "Thoughts? Or should I not even bother to ask?"

He cocked his head, examining the choice. "Not that one. It's too stuffy. Why do you even own it? It looks like something Darcy Minor would wear." Darcy was one of my harpy neighbors and seemed to be involved in every school fundraising event in Spellbound.

I sighed and placed the dress back in the closet. "Just choose one. I don't know why I bother to think for myself."

He rubbed his hands together and moved to review the contents of my closet. "There is that adorable skirt you bought at Ready-to-Were recently." He peered down the line of hangers until he spotted it. "There. That pale pink one."

I plucked the hanger from the rail. "I haven't worn it yet because I don't have a top to match." It was silly of me to buy a skirt when I had nothing to pair it with. I got caught up in the moment with Lucy and Ricardo, my local fashionistas.

"Nonsense," Gareth replied. "You've got that grey marl cowl neck top. It's perfect with the pleated skirt."

"Really?" I located the top in question and held it against me, along with the skirt. "Gareth, you're a genius. This looks amazing."

"Why would you ever doubt my expertise in these matters?"

"Shoes?"

He pointed to the set of charcoal kitten heels at the bottom of my closet on the shoe rack. "Those shoes were made for this outfit. It's fashion kismet."

I kissed his cheek. Well, I kissed the air that was his cheek. "Thanks, Gareth. You really are my guru."

"Nice to be useful. You know how feckless I feel."

"And we're working on that," I said, changing into my award-ready outfit. I slipped into the shoes and stood in front of Gareth for final inspection. "What do you think?"

Gareth tapped his cheek thoughtfully. "The outfit is lovely. It's the hair I'm worried about."

My shoulders sagged. "There's not much I can do about my hair. It is what it is."

He shook a finger at me. "It's attitudes like yours that halt the path to progress. Do you think your beloved George Washington looked at the troops across the Delaware River and simply threw up his hands in despair? *It is what it is, colonial rebels. Let's just accept defeat.*"

3

"Don't try to use my own country's history against me."

"I've had bags of time to read since my death. Why not show off?" He paused. "Why don't you wear your hair up for a change? You've a nice neck—not that I've noticed."

I hesitated. I couldn't tell him why wearing my hair up was a bad idea. That Daniel Starr, my best friend and the object of my affection, had discovered a birthmark on the nape of my neck—a blue star that signified my heritage as a sorceress rather than a run-of-the-mill witch. Although Lady Weatherby and Professor Holmes knew about the birthmark, they hadn't placed its significance. Yet. Aside from Daniel and me, the Grey sisters were the only ones who knew the truth about my origin. As much as I wanted to tell Gareth, I couldn't risk my secret getting out. Not that Gareth was capable of talking to anyone except Lyra and me.

"I think my hair would look too formal if it were up," I finally said. "Maybe a few loose curls. Something casual."

Gareth shrugged. "Suit yourself. Is there a spell you can do? You haven't much time."

"As a matter of fact there is. Begonia taught it to me in the secret lair."

"I thought it was all pillow fights and nail polish in that secret lair of yours."

"Careful Gareth," I warned. "You're sounding mighty heterosexual right now."

He clucked his tongue. "Well, we wouldn't want that now, would we?"

I walked into the bathroom and retrieved my wand from the counter. I focused my will and said, "Diamond and pearl/make this hair curl."

Gareth burst into fits of laughter as every hair on my head twisted into tiny corkscrew curls.

"You look like the backside of a poodle," he said, doubled over.

My jaw tensed. "Okay, that was a bit too much."

"You think?" Gareth said.

"That's enough from the Scottish chorus, thank you." I focused my will again and said, "Diamonds and pearls/relax these curls."

The corkscrews loosened and left me with gentle waves. Gareth made an approving noise at the back of his throat.

"Finally we agree on something," I said.

"I'll alert the Spellbound Gazette."

The wind chimes sounded. "The girls are here," I said excitedly. My remedial witch classmates had agreed to escort me to the ceremony.

"A shame that Daniel couldn't be the one to accompany you," Gareth said.

My expression hardened. "We agreed not to talk about that."

Daniel was now engaged to the mayor's daughter, Elsa Knightsbridge. Ever since their engagement, Elsa had made it abundantly clear that she preferred for Daniel not to spend time in mixed company, including me. Although I'd hoped that the fallen angel would choose me once he'd finally restored his halo, he made a left turn when I least expected it and reunited with his former girlfriend. Although I awoke with the painful knowledge every morning and went to sleep with it every night, I tried to wear a brave face for the rest of the world. After all, I had friends to care for and a job to do. I couldn't let my feelings for Daniel ruin the life I'd built here or I'd have nothing left at all.

"I wish *you* could be there today," I said.

Gareth smiled, not quite enough to show his fangs. "Same. You'll tell me about it, though, when you get back. I want all the gossip. Make sure you note the most hideous outfit so we can laugh."

I gave him a pointed look. "So *you* can laugh. That's not my style."

"No, it really isn't." He paused. "And I must admit, it is one of the things I admire most about you."

I peered at Gareth over my shoulder as I went to retrieve my handbag. "Gareth, you're not getting soft on me, are you? I need the surly Scotsman I've come to know and annoy."

"Don't forget your lipstick," he said. "And don't wear that bright pink shade. It makes you look like a clown harlot."

"There he is," I said in my most affectionate tone and blew him a parting kiss.

The grounds of the Mayor's Mansion were simply breathtaking. Gently rolling hills. A pond inhabited by ducks and swans. A picture-perfect white gazebo. It would have been a wonderland for children. As far as I knew, Elsa Knightsbridge was an only child. No wonder she was so spoiled. To have all this to yourself—how could it not color your view of the world? I felt entitled just standing here.

Today there were white ribbons and white balloons decorating the area around the gazebo, where I was to receive the ceremonial key. I saw Mayor Knightsbridge hovering by the microphone. She wore a sparkling pink suit and her wings rustled gently in the breeze. My friend Lucy stood beside her. They appeared to be reviewing notes for the ceremony. Lucy was the mayor's assistant and her very capable right hand. She gave an enthusiastic wave when she spotted me.

"Gosh, Emma, you make a pretty picture," Lucy said, making a beeline for me. "Your hair looks better than I've ever seen it."

"Thanks." Take that, Gareth.

"Here's how today will go," she said, shifting into business mode. "Once the clock strikes two, the mayor will give a short speech. You'll wait down here in the first row until she's ready to present you with the key."

"First row. Got it." The crowd had already gathered and my nerves began to creep to the surface.

"Are you okay?" Lucy asked. "Did you take your anti-anxiety potion this morning?"

My pulse quickened. "Oh no. In all the excitement of getting ready, I completely forgot."

Lucy bit her lip. "Should I send someone to get it?"

I waved her off. "No, no. It's too late now. I'll be fine. This is a happy occasion."

"Yes, but happy doesn't make you less anxious."

"I can go back and get it for you," Sophie volunteered.

The mayor tapped the microphone. "If everyone would please take a seat, we can get started."

I shot a panicked look at Sophie. "Not to worry. I'm sure it will be fine. It's just a key."

Lucy guided me to a seat in the first row, where the rest of the town council members were seated. Each one greeted me with either a nod or a smile—Wayne Stone, Lady J.R. Weatherby, Maeve McCullen, Juliet Montlake, and Lorenzo Mancini. Lord Gilder sat beside me. The head of the vampire coven was highly respected and an influential man in town.

"Welcome residents of Spellbound. Today we gather to celebrate a new member of our community. Someone who has proven her worth in a relatively short period of time."

I shifted uncomfortably in my seat. I never realized how difficult it was to accept praise until this moment. I simply wasn't accustomed to it. Although my grandparents loved me, they were lean on praise, and I was too young to remember compliments from my parents. My mother died when I was only three and my father died when I was seven. I had a few vague memories of him telling me that I'd done a good job or something similar, but nothing stood out. To hear the mayor's effusive praise now made my stomach churn. Instinctively, I craned my neck to search for Daniel. He was always my port in a storm. I jerked my head forward. What was I thinking? Daniel wasn't my port anymore. He was Elsa's. The sooner I accepted it, the happier I'd be.

"Miss Emma Hart came to us from the human world. It was our good fortune that she crossed the Spellbound border not knowing that she is a witch. I think we can all agree that the human world's loss is our gain." There was a scattering of applause and the mayor continued. "For her service to the community and her assistance in returning the town council members to their rightful selves, I am honored to present Miss Hart with the ceremonial key to Spellbound."

Everyone clapped as Lucy handed the mayor a large golden key about the size of a dachshund. The golden key sparkled in the sunlight. For an oversized prop, it was actually quite pretty. I figured I'd hang it on the wall in the foyer of the house. I knew Gareth wouldn't object to sparkly objects. After all, he was the one who'd hung a disco ball above his coffin.

Lord Gilder nudged me. "That's your cue."

"Oh, right." I stood and walked up the steps of the gazebo to accept my award.

"And now a few words from Miss Hart," the mayor said.

I froze beside her. A speech? I didn't know I was supposed to say anything. Panic rose in my throat. It was one thing to speak in front of a small group, but it was quite another to give a speech at a microphone in front of hundreds of critical eyes. I quickly scanned the crowd for friendly faces. Unfortunately, my gaze alighted on the two people I least wanted to see—Daniel and Elsa. My heart sank like a stone when I realized he wasn't even looking in my direction. Those turquoise eyes were fixed adoringly on Elsa and she was giggling like a teenager. She was snuggled against him, her arm looped through his. Tears stung my eyes. This was a special day and I didn't want them to ruin it. In my experience, special days were too few and far between.

What to say? I cleared my throat and stepped up to the microphone. "Thank you, Mayor Knightsbridge and members of the town council. It was my pleasure to help restore you to your normal, responsible selves." I became distracted by the sight of Elsa nibbling on Daniel's neck. He leaned over to whisper something to her and she took the opportunity to show her affection. A wave of nausea slammed into me. I averted my gaze and struggled to find someone else to fixate on. From her place in the front row, Lady Weatherby stared at me, her dark eyes glittering like two stones. She seemed to be daring me to fail.

"I know I haven't been here very long, but you have all welcomed me with open arms. I'm grateful to have made so many new friends in such a short time. I hope that I continue to make you proud every day."

People began to applaud and I was about ready to declare victory when my stomach betrayed me. As Mayor Knightsbridge handed me the key, I promptly rewarded her by vomiting all over it.

CHAPTER 2

I MOVED QUIETLY around the library, trying not to draw attention to myself. For one thing, I was looking for books on sorcery and didn't want anyone wondering why. While I could pass it off as casual interest, I'd played enough poker to know that I didn't have the face for it. I walked around with a perpetual guilty expression when I had nothing to feel guilty about. In this case, though, I had something to hide. Ever since the Grey Sisters dropped the bombshell that I was a sorceress, I had to live with this awful secret. It was Daniel who warned me not to tell anyone in Spellbound. Apparently, sorceresses were a little higher up the supernatural food chain and he worried how residents would respond to the news. So I'd pretend to be a witch for my own safety and continue to mess up the coven's spells that weren't in my nature to learn.

The second reason I was trying not to draw attention to myself was because I was waiting for Gareth to appear. Desperate to combat the ennui forced upon him by death, he'd been practicing making appearances in places other than our house and office. Lyra Grey was proving herself to be an adept tutor and her new set of pearly whites and own pair of eyes seemed a small price to pay in exchange for her help. Hopefully the sisters' shared eye would soon be a relic of the past.

I had no clue where Gareth might turn up so I made an effort to stay close to the atrium and keep watch. Not that anyone else would be able to see him, but I didn't want to unnerve people by talking to the empty space in front of me.

I glanced at the titles on the shelf. *Sorcery Today*. *Good Sorceress, Bad Sorceress*. *Fear No Sorceress*. They all seemed equally intimidating.

"Hey there, Emma. You're here late."

A voice startled me and I whipped around to see Karen Duckworth, the vampire librarian. "Hi." I took a casual step away from the shelf.

"I didn't notice you come in. What a wonderful ceremony yesterday. Did you enjoy it?"

Did I enjoy watching Mayor Knightsbridge use her fairy wand to remove puke from the ceremonial key in front of a hundred spectators? Um, no.

"I enjoyed it right up until the end," I said.

Karen waved me off. "Nobody cared. It was charming. No one else would have had the nerve to throw up within a mile radius of Mayor Knightsbridge. It's one of the ways you're different from everyone else here."

I wasn't convinced that was a plus.

"Can I help you find anything?" she asked, checking her watch. "We'll be closing soon, so you may want to choose something."

"That's okay. I'm just browsing," I said. "There's still so much to learn. I like to see what catches my eye."

"You're in the right section," she said. "Lots of drama on these shelves. A lot of it reads like fiction." She leaned against one of the shelves and smiled. "Thanks for the tip about speed dating, by the way. I've been there a couple more times since we went together. It's fun."

"I'm glad," I said. "Any decent prospects?"

Her gaze drifted to the floor. "Maybe. I don't want to speak too soon and jinx it."

"I totally understand." Out of the corner of my eye, I saw Gareth materialize near the cooking section. Somehow, I doubted that was a coincidence. He saw me and gave a triumphant wave.

"I heard Markos asked you out," Karen said. "Good catch."

My cheeks colored. "I've agreed to a friendly outing. It's not a date." And if I didn't get home soon, I'd be late for his arrival.

She patted me on the back. "I know plenty of women who wouldn't mind a friendly outing with Markos. Maybe we can double date one of these days, if my guy pans out."

"I'd like that." Gareth gestured impatiently, as though I'd kept him waiting all this time. "I'm so sorry, but I need to go. It was nice catching up."

I hurried to the cooking section where Gareth was already admiring the books on the shelf. "Once I can touch things again with more regularity, I'm going to check out this entire row of cookbooks and show you how to make a real meal."

"I would think an expert like you wouldn't need a cook-book," I teased.

"I want you to be able to learn the steps," he said. "I know them by heart. It's not easy to teach that way. A practical guide is better."

"I find it boring to cook for one person," I said. "It feels like a waste of energy."

"You need to eat," he said. "Food gives you energy."

He was right. I hadn't been very good about taking care of myself. I'd been too distracted by Daniel's engagement. It was like a punch in the gut every time I thought about it and I promptly lost whatever appetite I'd managed to acquire.

"Speaking of food," I said. "I really need to get home. You took longer than I expected and I need to get ready for Markos."

"Fine," Gareth said glumly. "Race you back, shall I?"

"If your arrival here is any indication, I'll see you tomorrow."

He glared at me before disappearing. I hustled out of the library and drove home to change and freshen up. I was already downstairs and ready to go out again by the time Gareth made it home.

"Are you nervous for your date?" Gareth asked. "Because you look nervous."

I folded my arms. "First of all, it is not a date. I have made that very clear. Second of all, I do not look nervous. I look relaxed. Very, very relaxed."

"Then how do you explain that vein bulging from your forehead?" he asked. He pointed to a spot above my eyes.

"Hey, I felt that." Although I was happy to celebrate his victories, I wasn't too excited at the prospect of him poking me at will.

"Every day gets a wee bit better," he said. "By this time next year, who knows what I'll be capable of?"

"I know one fella who is extremely happy about your progress," I said, glancing down at Magpie. The hideous cat was twisting his body between Gareth's phantom legs. "Maybe one of these days, he'll actually feel your legs again."

The wind chimes sounded and I jumped.

Gareth laughed. "Oh no, you're not the least bit nervous. Do yourself a favor and try to have a good time."

My heart raced. "You'll be here when I get back, won't you? You're not going to try and materialize at the club again tonight?"

Gareth patted me on the head and I felt a slight breeze. "I promise I'll be here to listen to all the salacious details."

"There will be no salacious details," I called over my shoulder. I opened the door to greet Markos.

"No salacious details at all?" he asked good-naturedly. "How disappointing."

My cheeks reddened. "Sorry, I didn't mean for you to hear that." I forced a smile. "I'm ready when you are."

He eyed my sundress. "As much as I'd like to admire your bare shoulders for the duration of the evening, may I suggest a cardigan? We're going to be outside and it gets a little chilly once the sun goes down."

I warmed all over from the compliment and then instantly chastised myself. *This is not a date*. It didn't matter whether he wanted to admire my bare arms or not. Friendly outing only.

I turned to run upstairs and nearly ran smack into Sedgwick, my owl familiar, who held a lilac cardigan in his curved beak. "Thanks, Sedgwick." I took the cardigan and joined Markos on the front porch.

"You look pretty tonight, Emma," he said.

I had to admit, he looked pretty good himself. With his tall frame and muscles that Thor would envy, it was easy to forget he was actually a minotaur.

I bumped him gently with my elbow. "It's not a date, remember? It's a friendly outing."

He gave me a flirtatious wink. "What? Compliments are prohibited during a friendly outing? Forgive me. I didn't have a chance to review the Friendly Outing Rulebook before I left the house."

He walked to the driveway where his jalopy was parked, except it wasn't a jalopy at all. It reminded me of an Audi R8 —very sleek and even cooler because it was magical.

"So where's the mystery location?" I asked. He'd refused

to divulge the location of our outing when I asked him earlier. In fact, we'd exchanged multiple messages on the subject, which annoyed Sedgwick and Markos's owl to no end. Sedgwick was still convinced that he lost weight this week as a result of our constant communications.

"Patience, Emma. We're almost there."

We drove past the church and the casino to an area I hadn't seen before. There were fewer trees. I gasped at the sight of a field of colorful flowers. They reminded me of wildflowers—except they sparkled.

"How beautiful," I said. "What is this place?"

Markos glanced out the window and smiled. "You haven't been to Faraway Field?"

I shook my head. "I can't believe no one has told me about this place. It's incredible."

"Technically, the field belongs to me," Markos said. "But I don't restrict people. There's no such thing as trespassing at Faraway Field."

"Aren't you worried about people taking all the flowers or trampling them?" As altruistic as Markos sounded, I would still be worried about the destruction of the field over time.

"They're magical flowers, Emma," he said. "They simply grow back."

I swatted his arm playfully. "Regular flowers grow back, too. What's so special about that?"

He pulled the jalopy over to the side of the road. "Allow me to demonstrate." He got out of the car and walked to the edge of the field, plucking the nearest flower. It was bright purple and glimmered in the fading sunlight. No sooner had he uprooted the flower than another one appeared in its place.

My eyes popped. "Amazing."

He returned to the jalopy with the flower and handed it

to me. "If you think that's amazing, wait until you see what's next."

We continued a little bit further down the road until we reached what appeared to be a block of hedges. The sign read 'South East Labyrinth.'

"We're going into one of your labyrinths?" I asked. I'd heard a lot about them, but the closest I'd been to one was the inflatable kind for children.

"We're not just going to walk through it," he said. "We're going to have a picnic in it." He parked the jalopy and proceeded to open the trunk. When he came around to open my door, I noticed the wicker basket in his hand.

"Wow. A real picnic. I don't think I've ever had a picnic before."

His brow lifted in surprise. "No? I thought that was a very human activity."

"Our picnics in Pennsylvania consisted of backyard grills and hot dogs," I said. While I liked those two things very much, the idea of a traditional picnic intrigued me.

"The entrance is up ahead," he said. We walked until we arrived at the mouth of the labyrinth, where he reached for my hand.

I glanced at him. "Friendly outing," I reminded him.

He nodded toward the labyrinth. "Labyrinth," he replied.

Fair enough. I had no interest in getting lost tonight, so I didn't let go of his hand. If anything, I gripped it more tightly.

"Is it open to the public?" I asked.

"Typically, yes," he said. "But I closed it for tonight. Party of two only."

The beginning of the labyrinth seemed to comprise tall hedges. It was only once we started walking deeper into the maze that I realized the hedges behind us were shifting. My heart began to pound.

"The hedges are moving," I said. "Is that supposed to happen?"

Markos glanced calmly over his shoulder. "I hope so since I designed it that way. No need to worry. I know every inch of this place."

"I'm glad one of us does."

We enter the clearing where the hedges were brightened by tiny fairy lights. The ground was covered in soft, silky grass, the kind you wanted to roll around in. It smelled like lazy spring mornings.

"I thought we could eat here, if that's okay with you," Markos said.

I glanced around the clearing. It was more romantic than I was expecting. Still, it was very pretty and it seemed that Markos had put a lot of thought into our outing.

"This spot is perfect." Not to mention I was starving. I'd barely eaten all day thanks to my nerves.

Markos snapped his fingers and the basket opened. A large blanket floated out and unfolded on the ground beside us.

"An enchanted picnic basket?" I queried.

He nodded. "You haven't seen one of these yet?"

I shook my head. "First time."

He snapped his fingers again and a bottle of wine popped out of the basket. "I don't know who's been showing you around town, but they haven't done such a hot job." He sat on the blanket and patted the spot beside him. "What would be your ideal picnic food?"

I tried to think. It wasn't a question I'd encountered before, given that I'd never been on a real picnic. "I guess I see fried chicken in movies when people have a picnic."

"Never mind what you've seen. I want to know what *your* ideal picnic is."

I touched my cheek thoughtfully. "I have to be honest. As

much as I like the idea of a traditional picnic, I really miss hot dogs on the grill in summer." In fact, it was one of my favorite memories from childhood. The smell of food cooking on a grill. We would occasionally get invited to a barbecue and the smell would stay with me for weeks afterward.

"Mustard or ketchup?" he asked.

"What type of heathen do you take me for? Mustard, of course."

He snapped his fingers and a jumbo beef hot dog on a bun drifted out of the basket. The streak of mustard across the middle caught my eye. It even had the blackened grill marks, just the way I liked it. I plucked it from the air when it came close enough.

"Markos, this is fantastic. Thank you so much." I took a generous bite and moaned gently.

He gave me a crooked smile. "I like that sound. Can you do it again?"

I immediately became self-conscious. "What about you? What will you be having?"

Markos snapped his fingers and the plate came flying out of the basket, complete with a porterhouse steak. A knife and fork quickly followed.

"Fancy," I said. "Do you consider premium steak a picnic staple?"

"It is for me," he said. "Can I offer you any wine? Or water? I have both."

"I wouldn't mind a small glass of wine," I said.

He was in the process of uncorking the bottle when his owl appeared. He glanced up in surprise. "Larry, what are you doing here?"

The owl dropped a message into his lap, narrowly avoiding the steak. Markos scanned the note and his expression darkened. "I'm terribly sorry, Emma, but we need to go. I promise I'll make it up to you."

I wolfed down the last bite of my hot dog. "Is something wrong?"

"It's my new office building. They just discovered a body there. I need to go now."

A body? "That's awful."

"I'll drop you home first before I head over there," he said.

"Didn't you say your new headquarters is on the eastern edge of town?" I asked. "It's completely out of the way to take me home first. I'll come with you."

"Are you sure?" he asked, uncertain.

"Absolutely."

He snapped his fingers and the entire picnic disappeared back into the basket. "It's not much of a date, is it? If I take you to see a dead body."

"Doesn't matter since it's not a date anyway," I reminded him gently.

He smiled down at me and took my hand. "So you keep telling me. Okay, let's go."

CHAPTER 3

BY THE TIME WE ARRIVED, there were several people on the scene. I waved to Boyd, the druid healer. Maybe they thought the person was still alive when they found him. That would be the only reason to call Boyd. A healer was no good to a dead person.

We entered the lobby of the building where I paused to admire the high ceiling.

"How tall is this atrium?" I asked. It seemed much taller than the one in the library.

"It's ten stories tall," Markos said proudly. "I wanted to make sure it was the tallest atrium in Spellbound, so I had my guys measure all of the others first and then added another few stories for good measure."

Impressive. It wasn't only tall, but it was designed to look like there was no ceiling at all, as though the building simply ceased to exist and blended into the sky.

"If I didn't know any better, I'd say you used magic," I said.

"Nope," he said, his hands on his hips. "This is pure, old-fashioned architecture."

The body was gone by the time we arrived at the scene,

transported to the coroner's office. Astrid, the new Valkyrie sheriff, was there, her face scrunched up in concentration. She looked surprised to see me.

"What happened?" Markos asked, frowning. "Who is it?"

"Ed Doyle," Astrid replied. I didn't recognize the name.

Markos choked. "The building inspector?"

Astrid touched the ladder that leaned against the wall. "It looks like he might have been on his way down when one of the rungs broke. He fell from up there." She pointed upward, near the top of the ladder. "Boyd thinks he broke his neck when he hit the floor."

Markos closed his eyes briefly. "Was anyone here? Did anyone see what happened?"

Astrid jerked her thumb. "Your janitor found him. He's in the kitchen if you want to speak with him. We asked him to stick around for additional questions."

"Yes, I'll speak to him now. Poor Milo. It must've been quite a shock."

I followed Markos to the office kitchen. With an enormous stainless steel double sink and sleek countertops, it was more like a chef's kitchen than any office kitchen I'd ever seen. Milo sat at the table, his head in his hands. Markos clapped him on the shoulder.

"How are you holding up, Milo?"

Milo peered up at him, his face ashen. "I was almost finished for the evening, boss. I had just rounded the corner when I heard him yell. I didn't see him fall, but by the time I got there, he was on the floor. I thought maybe he had a pulse, but I wasn't sure."

"No one else was here?" Markos asked.

Milo shook his head. "Just me. I knew someone else was here, though, because I'd seen a jalopy full of equipment out front."

"Can I get you a drink, Milo?" I asked. "Have you had any water recently?"

Milo gave me an appreciative nod. "Water sounds good, thanks."

I retrieved a glass from the cabinet and filled it was water from the tap. He gulped it down greedily.

"If Sheriff Astrid is finished with you, I want you to go home and get a good night's sleep," Markos said. "Don't worry about coming in tomorrow."

"Are you sure, boss?" Milo asked.

Markos squeezed his arm gently. "You're a valued member of the team, Milo. I don't want you coming in here feeling traumatized. Take a break."

Milo wiped his mouth with the back of his hand. "I am mighty tired. It was such a shock. I've never seen a dead body before, except at a funeral."

"Let me see if Sheriff Astrid has any more questions," I offered. I went back to the place where the body was found. Astrid was still there, examining the ladder.

"Milo is pretty tired," I said. "Can we send him home?"

"Sure. I think we have everything we need from him for now." She continued to study the broken rung.

"What's the matter?" I knew Astrid well enough to recognize her facial expressions. Something wasn't sitting right with her.

"It's the rung. The marks on it. They don't fit with normal wear and tear."

"Ed is a satyr. Could his hooves have broken the rung?"

"Ed is the Spellbound building inspector," Astrid said. "This is his ladder. It's designed for his hooves. No, the marks look to me like someone tampered with it before he used it."

My eyes widened. "You don't think this was an accident?"

Astrid ran her fingers along the broken piece of ladder.

"No. In fact, the more I look at this, the more I'm convinced that this was murder."

A murder in Markos's new corporate headquarters? The minotaur was not going to be happy about this.

"Was Ed only here today?" I asked.

"I'm not sure," Astrid said. "These are questions I'm going to have for Markos. I assume your date is over now." She gave me a pointed look.

"It's not a date," I said. "Just a friendly outing."

Astrid suppressed a smile. "Whatever you say."

Markos appeared from the kitchen. "I sent Milo home, if that's okay. I figured if you need him, you know where to find him."

Astrid nodded. "It's fine. I have questions for you, if you have a few minutes."

I looked uneasily at Markos.

"I have all the time you need," Markos said. "Why don't we sit in the kitchen where it's more comfortable?"

"To be fair, everywhere in your office looks comfortable," Astrid said.

"Thank you," he replied. "That was one of the goals."

We returned to the kitchen and Markos and I sat across from Astrid.

"How well did you know Ed?" Astrid asked.

"Fairly well. Ed has inspected all of my designs," Markos said. "I've known him for years."

"And did you get along?"

"Mostly," he said.

"What was his schedule today? Do you know when he arrived?"

"I saw him this afternoon." Markos scratched his chin thoughtfully. "He was here yesterday evening as well."

"Does it typically take more than a day for an inspection?" Astrid asked.

Markos shrugged. "It does for my buildings. They're not your standard designs."

"True." Astrid drummed her fingers on the table. "Who else was here when Ed was here?"

"I'll need to check the log," Markos said. "Can I get it to you tomorrow?"

"Sure."

"Anything else?" Markos asked. "I should probably escort Emma home."

"No, that's good enough for now. Thanks." Astrid scraped back her chair and stood. "Any chance you could drop me off at the station? I caught a ride here with the transport team."

"No problem," Markos replied.

"I'd love to see the rest of the building another time," I said, glancing around as we left. "It's amazing."

Markos brightened. "I'd love to show it to you. We'll arrange another…outing."

As much as I told myself it was the opportunity to make a new friend, deep down I knew my intentions were less pure. Markos was a welcome distraction from Daniel's engagement. He seemed to know it, too, but was too kind to mention it.

I sighed. He almost seemed too good to be true.

I didn't love the idea of therapy. It wasn't easy to trust someone with your innermost secrets. I was already regretting that Daniel knew the secret about my origin, especially now that he was engaged to Elsa Knightsbridge. While I still trusted Daniel, the trust did not come as easily as it once had. I remained baffled by his sudden change of heart. Never mind the fact that I was in love with him. Even without that pesky minor detail, I would still be scratching my head over his recent life-changing decision.

The waiting room was minimal. A single couch. A coffee table. A magazine rack with outdated publications. Not even a receptionist. I only knew that I wasn't alone in the office because I heard voices behind the closed door. They were muffled so I couldn't actually understand what was being said. Probably a good thing considering this was a therapist's office and all conversations were, or should be, private.

The door finally opened and a woman called to me from inside the room. "Is that you, Emma Hart? Come on in."

I was surprised to enter and discover that my therapist was the only one there.

"Miss Hall? I heard voices," I said. "I thought you were in a session with a client."

Catherine Hall smiled. "Oh, there was. You exit via a different door. That preserves the identity of my clients should they desire it."

"Good to know." I took in the room's decor. It was not at all what I was expecting. There was a chaise lounge and a chair, but there was also a bar with two stools and music playing in the background. Not relaxing music, though. More like alternative rock. It was low enough to allow us to talk and be heard, but loud enough to make you want to move your feet to the beat.

"But it's Dr. Hall or just plain Catherine, if you prefer. I didn't suffer through years at Vampire University to be called Miss."

"Of course not. I'm sorry. I didn't realize."

Catherine moved behind the bar and poured herself a drink. "What's your poison?" She waved me off. "Wait, let me guess." She proceeded to assess me. "I'm going to go with something tooth-achingly sweet. Lord of Darkness, please don't say barberry-tini or we may have to part company here and now."

"To be honest, I haven't sampled enough drinks here to

have a favorite yet." I hesitated. "Are you sure that drinking during a session is a good idea?"

Catherine began to prepare me a drink with the expert precision of a bartender. "I find it helps relax my client."

"Then why do you have a drink, too?" I asked, eyeing the mug of ale on the counter.

"Sweetheart, nobody likes to drink alone."

"What's that you're drinking?" I asked. The ale looked frothy and refreshing.

Catherine took a generous sip. "This is one of my favorites. It's called Nasty Woman."

"Maybe I'll try that next time." If there was a next time.

Catherine gestured for me to sit. "Anywhere you like. If you prefer the chair, I'm happy to take the lounger."

I took the chair. "And what about the music? Do we need to turn that off?"

Catherine scrutinized me. "You don't like music? What's wrong with you?" She tilted her head back and laughed. "I guess I'll figure that out soon enough."

I was taken aback. "I didn't say I don't like music. I was just wondering whether it was appropriate to have it on during our session."

Catherine clapped her hands. "Music off."

The background fell silent. She gave me a look that said *happy now?* She handed me a glass with a deep purple liquid.

"Is this a barberry-tini?" I asked.

"Hell no. I fixed you a Bitter Pill. Now go ahead and swallow it."

That sounded…challenging.

"So what brings you here?" she asked. "You must have something on your mind." Catherine joined me, seating herself on the chaise lounge.

"My assistant at work suggested I might want to speak to someone. I have a lot of stress in my life right now."

"You mean because that angelic bastard Daniel Starr is engaged to Elsa, the magical bitch fairy?"

I stiffened. "What does that have to do with anything?"

Catherine gave me a sympathetic smile. "Honey, please. You are a walking, talking ball of emotion. Your love for him is written all over you. Like the plague. A love plague. Why do you think I'm sitting over here? Wouldn't want to catch it."

I didn't think that was true. In fact, I did my very best to keep my feelings to myself because I didn't want to burden others with the knowledge and make them uncomfortable.

I narrowed my eyes. "Who told you?"

Catherine sighed loudly. "Okay, fine. I heard it second-hand from someone in town. But the question clearly irritated you, so I have to assume it's true."

I glanced away, unwilling to meet her gaze. "Yes, it's true. But that isn't why I'm here. There's nothing I can do about Daniel. He's made his choice."

"People don't come to therapy because they intend to *do* anything," she said. "Sometimes it just helps to talk about how you're feeling. Even if that means you're feeling horrible because there's nothing you can do about a situation. Take Spellbound. You've been trapped here against your will, just like the rest of us. How does that make you feel?"

"It depends," I said. "Some days are better than others. I'm happy to have met so many wonderful friends. I didn't have relationships like this in the human world."

"Good grief, Pollyanna. Is this shtick for real?"

I stared at her. "There's no shtick."

"So you really feel blessed to be here because you were shunned in the human world?"

"Not shunned…"

"I find it hard to believe a pretty girl like you had no friends. I mean, I didn't have many friends in the human world because I couldn't seem to stop eating them, but that's a different story."

I inched my chair away from her as imperceptibly as I could. "I wasn't a pariah or anything. I just tended to keep to myself. I'd been hurt a lot and I felt it was best not to get close to people."

"Because you were afraid they would leave you like your parents did?"

I bristled. "Technically, they didn't leave me. They died."

"And no departure is more permanent."

Unless you were a Scottish vampire.

Catherine swilled her ale. "So is that what you're hung up on? Your parents' death?"

I folded my hands in my lap. "I don't want to talk about it."

"No? Okay then. You don't want to talk about your unrequited love for Daniel or your parents' death. What do you want to talk about?"

I glanced around the room, uncertain. "How about the weather? Why is it always perfect here yet plants and flowers manage to grow?"

"The spell, honey. Next question."

"Did you attend my special ceremony?" I asked.

"You want to talk about your nervous stomach?" She blew a raspberry. "Boring. Next topic."

"I wasn't aware that my topics of conversation needed to interest you."

"Well, it certainly helps." She eyed my half empty glass. "How's your drink?"

"Not bad, actually."

"New favorite?"

"I wouldn't say that."

She set her empty mug on the coffee table. "How do you

like living with a vampire ghost? He's a real pain in the ass, isn't he?"

"Did you know Gareth?"

She rolled her eyes. "I'm a vampire in Spellbound. Of course I knew Gareth."

"He suggested I make an appointment with Thalia," I said, referring to the therapist in the office across the hall.

Catherine snorted. "I'll bet. Why didn't you?"

"I think you know why."

"Because she's booked from now until Hades comes, but my schedule has immediate availability. Is that right?"

I decided to be honest. "Pretty much."

"That's because she's so nice. It's nauseating. People think her niceness helps them, but it really doesn't."

"No?"

"Of course not. Clients need raw, unfiltered honesty. Not drivel." She stood to refill her mug. "The reason she's so booked up is because her clients have been going to her for years. Eventually, they shouldn't need her anymore. She should have room for fresh blood." She sighed dreamily. "Fresh blood."

"You advocate the tough love approach?" I queried.

"Maybe." She paused. "That was your grandmother, I take it?"

"What was?"

"Tough love."

I stared at a fixed point on the wall. "Maybe."

She poured another glass of ale. "Not to worry, Emma. I think you and I will get along swimmingly."

I gulped. I was glad one of us was confident because I sure wasn't.

"Let's talk about your grandmother," she said.

So we did.

CHAPTER 4

I MET Astrid outside Ed Doyle's beige ranch-style house. As the new deputy, her sister was supposed to join her, but Britta was apparently hung over from a night out with werewolves and unable to make her legs work properly.

"Thanks for coming," Astrid said. "I'm sure you have better things to do."

"That's okay," I said. "I don't want to see Markos have any trouble. He's really excited about his new office."

"Agreed. The sooner we can wrap this up, the better."

Astrid picked the lock on the door with a magical pin and opened the door. "Ed was a decent guy. I ran into him around town now and again. Fairly serious, but I never heard him say a bad word about anybody."

The inside of the house was as plain as the outside. White walls. Nondescript carpet. There was no personality injected into the decor whatsoever.

We split up—Astrid took the bedroom and I took the living room. There was nothing out of place. No evidence that anyone had come looking for an item. A single shelf hung on the wall, covered in what appeared to be bowling trophies. There were several books on the end table next to the couch. I thumbed through them to see if they belonged to the library. The stickler in me wanted to make sure they were returned in a timely manner. On the whole, it seemed like a very typical bachelor pad. Slightly messy and no personal effects such as framed photos or tokens of affection.

Astrid emerged from the bedroom. "Anything in here? The bedroom is dullsville. Poor guy. Not much of a personal life."

"Nothing sticks out in here," I said. "He seems to like crossword puzzles." I'd noticed those on the table next to the recliner. I suspected that was where Ed spent many hours of his leisure time.

"There doesn't seem to be any old girlfriends or boyfriends to question," Astrid said.

"I guess that explains the dull bedroom," I said. "Nothing noteworthy in the closet?" In my experience, the contents of a closet could tell you a lot about a person. It was how I discovered Gareth's well-kept secret. At least it wasn't a well-kept secret anymore.

"It's too bad you can't see everyone's ghosts," Astrid said. "I mean you're handy enough as it is, but imagine the possibilities."

I laughed. "Then I think the council would have to find a new public defender. I'd be too busy communing with the other side."

"That could be your own business," Astrid said. "You'd be like Kassandra except without the funky style."

"I don't know," I said. "Kassandra's abilities are more limited than mine, at least in terms of Gareth. She needed to channel him through something. She couldn't see him easily the way I can."

Astrid tilted her head. "Why do you think that is?"

I quickly realized that I'd said too much. I didn't want my

friends questioning the extent of my abilities to the point that they realized I was more than a coven witch. They seemed to like Emma the Witch, but who knew how they would feel about Emma the Sorceress. Based on the town's history with the enchantress, I didn't think it would go over very well.

"I'll check the bathroom. You check the kitchen," Astrid said. "I'm glad he didn't have any pets. That's the worst when you walk in the house and realize that no one's taking care of the animal."

Like Magpie. If I hadn't turned up at Gareth's house, I had no idea what would have become of Magpie. That being said, he was a feisty cat with no intention of becoming a victim of circumstance. Heck, Magpie refused to lose a battle with a floating feather. He certainly wouldn't have given up on life if I hadn't moved in.

I opened kitchen cabinets and drawers searching for any scrap of useful information. He certainly had a lot of tools, which made sense for a building inspector. He also kept a stack of notebooks on a desk in the kitchen. I rifled through them and realized that they were notes from previous jobs. I started with the most recent entries to see if he'd made any significant notes. We could cross-reference his notebooks with the reports he filed at the office.

"The only information I learned in the bathroom is that Ed is a typical bachelor," Astrid said. "Or was."

"Not much of a cleaner, huh?" I asked, still reviewing one of the notebooks.

Astrid joined me at the small desk. "What are these?"

"His own notes on previous jobs. Maybe we'll come across a disgruntled building owner."

"Here's something interesting," Astrid said. "He seems to have had a disagreement with George recently."

"The Yeti?"

"Yeah. I wonder if he reported this to the office."

"Easy enough to check."

"Either way, it'll be a good excuse to grab an ice cream cone," she said.

I shot her a look of surprise. "Who needs an excuse for ice cream?"

After confirming the notes in the town's administrative office, Astrid and I headed over to Icebergs to speak with George. I'd never met a Yeti before and was curious to see what he looked like.

"So does George keep a human form like Markos and the harpies?" I asked.

Astrid squinted at me. "No, why would he do a thing like that?"

I shrugged. "I don't know. Why do the harpies? Why does Markos?"

"Have you seen the harpies in their native forms? We should be thankful they walk around most of the time as humans."

"What about Markos? Have you ever seen him in his minotaur form?" I wondered whether he was as intimidating as I imagined.

"If you're wondering whether you'd want to date him in his minotaur form, I suspect the answer is no."

"I don't want to date him in his human form either," I insisted.

"Then you should really cut bait because he is definitely interested," Astrid said. "My sister won't shut up about it. She accuses you of hoarding eligible bachelors."

I couldn't help but laugh. I was the girl who never had a date in high school. I had more unrequited crushes than I could count on both hands. That any woman should be jealous of me seemed patently absurd.

Astrid pushed open the door to the ice cream shop and a bell jingled. The place was empty except for George. He stood behind the counter reading the Spellbound Gazette. He was easily seven feet tall with a body covered in white fur. He reminded me of the abominable snowman from the *Rudolph the Red-Nosed Reindeer* movie.

He set the paper down on the counter when we approached. "Hey there, Astrid. Sorry, I guess it's Sheriff Astrid now. Congrats on that promotion, by the way."

"Thanks, George. What time do you open?"

George glanced at the clock on the wall. "Another hour, but I get the sense you two aren't here for the ice cream."

"What makes you say that?" Astrid asked.

George smiled and I noticed how perfectly square his teeth were. Not a meat eater then. "You're wearing your 'official business face.'" He glanced at me. "You must be the new lawyer. Gareth's replacement."

"Emma Hart," I said, and held out my hand. He shook it and I was surprised by the softness of the skin on his hand. The top end was covered in white fur, but the palm was smooth.

"We're here to talk to you about Ed Doyle," Astrid said.

George's furry forehead lifted. "The building inspector? I heard he fell off a ladder during a job." He shook his head. "It's a real shame. He was a nice fella."

Astrid cocked her head. "You think so? It didn't bother you when he cited you for code violations last month?"

George looked taken aback. "Well, I was surprised. As far as I knew, everything was up to code."

"I heard you had to close the shop for a few days until the repairs could be made," Astrid said. "You must've lost some business."

"Of course I lost business. The weather's been a few degrees warmer. Folks want their ice cream and water ice."

Astrid leaned forward. "That must've really pissed you off."

"I was more annoyed than angry, if that's what you're asking." George glanced from Astrid to me. "You don't think I had anything to do with Ed's death, do you? He fell off a ladder."

"He fell off a ladder because someone tampered with one of the rungs," Astrid explained.

George's blue eyes widened. "The satyr was murdered?"

"It seems so," Astrid said.

George whistled. "Holy icebergs. I wasn't expecting to hear that. Is it possible that the ladder was simply faulty?"

"Not based on the evidence," Astrid said. "When was the last time you saw Ed?"

George scratched his furry face. "Gosh, I don't think I've seen him since his final visit here to sign off on the repairs."

"And you haven't seen his jalopy anywhere?" she persisted. "It's pretty obvious with all of the tools and the ladder on the top."

George shook his head. "If I saw it, then it didn't register. Then again, I wasn't looking for him. Once we were up and running, I can't say I thought about him again."

"So you weren't holding a grudge?" Astrid asked.

"Absolutely not," George replied. "In fact, I'm pretty sure I gave him a few coupons for free water ice."

"Thanks for your time, George," Astrid said.

"No problem. Can I interest you ladies in anything on the menu?" he asked. "I've got blueberry tart water ice that's out of this world."

"I wouldn't mind a scoop of Pixie Rainbow," Astrid said.

George broke into a broad smile. "I should have known. I

don't think you've ever ordered anything else." He looked at me. "And for you, Miss Lawyer?"

"It's all new to me," I said. And it looked amazing. Every flavor seemed to burst with wonderful possibility. "What do you recommend?"

George tapped his furry fingers on the counter. "I'm always coming up with new flavors and trying them out. I'm experimenting with a burstberry blend if you'd like to try it."

I chewed my lip, debating. "Do you have anything with chocolate? I'm partial to chocolate ice cream, but I'd like to try something different."

George lit up. "I have the perfect thing." He touched the large menu on the wall behind his head. "Sorceress on a Stick. It's like a Fudgsicle-style ice cream with ribbons of caramel."

"Why is it called Sorceress on a Stick?" I asked.

"Because you eat off a stick instead of a cone and the ice cream is dark, like her magic."

I felt the heat rise to my cheeks. "I think I'll try the Unicorn's Horn." It was vanilla ice cream coated in white chocolate on a popsicle stick.

"That's a good choice, too," George said. He scooped Astrid's cup first and then took care of my order.

When Astrid reached into her pocket, he waved her off. "I have to pay, George, or there's an appearance of impropriety."

"Fine, just pay for yours," he relented. "But not Emma's. There's no impropriety there."

Astrid handed him a few coins.

"Thanks, George," I said, licking away happily. "This is delicious."

"Glad to hear it," he said. "Let me know if you have any more questions about Ed. I'm sorry I wasn't very helpful."

"You were helpful, George," Astrid reassured him. "Anyone who answers my questions honestly is helpful."

George smiled. "Good luck with the investigation."

"Thanks," Astrid said.

I tried to say goodbye, but my mouth was too full of ice cream. No matter. After tasting this delicious concoction, I knew I'd be back.

CHAPTER 5

THE INVITATION DID NOT ARRIVE by owl. Instead it came via Elf Express, with an elf dressed as a footman, arriving in a Cinderella-style carriage. If this was how Elsa chose to deliver the invitations for the engagement party, I could only imagine what the wedding would be like.

Oh, I guess they're too good for an owl, Sedgwick complained. He was perched on the porch overhang, observing the spectacle.

I'm surprised to be getting an invitation at all, I said. Since Mayor Knightsbridge was footing the bill, though, I suspected she played a role in my inclusion. She was as eager to end this engagement as I was.

I stood on the front step below, awaiting the footman's arrival.

"Good morning, Henry," I said, as he climbed down from the carriage. "I imagine you're quite busy today. Must have a lot of invitations to deliver."

Henry mustered a smile, twitching in his uncomfortable and ridiculous outfit. He blew the pink plume away from his forehead and tried to focus on me.

"She's paying us double, so I can't complain." He handed me the invitation. It was, unsurprisingly, the most decadent invitation I'd ever seen. The paper was dusted with gold and silver and the calligraphy was the most fabulous scrawl imaginable. No left-handed resident was responsible for that work of art.

"Word of advice," Henry said. "Stand back a little when you open it. Otherwise, you'll be in for a big surprise." He gave me a wave and started back to his carriage.

"Would you like to come in for a drink?" I offered.

"I'd love to stay and chat, but I've got heaps more to deliver. It's the party of the season, apparently." He started the carriage and disappeared down the road.

I took Henry's advice and held the invitation at arm's length when I opened it. A white dove flew out, sprinkling fairy dust as it shot upward and disappeared into the sky.

Sedgwick groaned. *Money doesn't buy you class.*

The party was to be held at the Mayor's Mansion next Friday at eight. It definitely seemed like it was going to be a grand affair.

At least you can bring a date, Sedgwick observed.

He was right. The envelope was addressed to Miss Emma Hart and Guest.

You should have Demetrius escort you, Sedgwick said. *Daniel will hate that.*

"I wish Gareth could come," I said. "Or maybe it would be better to go alone."

Only if you want to spend the evening crying in a corner, Sedgwick said. *Which I wouldn't put past you.*

I folded the invitation and retreated into the house. "You're probably right. I'll have to think about it."

And you'll need an amazing dress, Sedgwick said. He perched on the banister.

"Since when do you care whether I look good?" I asked.

It isn't so much that I care, Sedgwick said. *I only want to put Daniel and Elsa in their place. The more amazing you look, the more likely that is to happen.*

"You only want revenge because they chose not to use an owl for delivery," I chastised him.

Or maybe I don't want to see you wallow in self-pity for the next decade. Your nighttime crying keeps me awake.

I became slightly self-conscious at the thought of Sedgwick listening to me cry at night. "I'm sorry, Sedgwick. Sometimes I can't help it. I start thinking…"

Don't start thinking now or the waterworks will erupt, he interjected.

I glanced around the empty foyer. "Have you seen Gareth? I would've thought he'd come running at the sight of a bedazzled carriage out front."

He mentioned something about trying to materialize in the country club, Sedgwick said.

That explained it. I was glad Gareth seemed to have found a purpose. It was better than having him sulking around the house all day.

I headed upstairs and left the invitation on my bedroom dresser. I didn't want to decide right away. Part of me was convinced I should just stay home—that I would find the whole ordeal too painful.

Gareth drifted into the room, startling me.

"Gareth," I cried. "You can't sneak up on a person like that."

"You already know you have a ghost," he said. "It's not like I can make loud footsteps. Not yet anyway."

I sat down on the bed and my shoulders sagged. "You're right. I'm sorry."

He spotted the invitation on the dresser and went over to investigate. "What's this?"

"You missed the spectacle," I said. "It's the invitation to Daniel and Elsa's engagement party."

He whistled. "I best start practicing now to materialize in the Mayor's Mansion."

"I would love it if you could," I said. "Did you have any luck with the country club?"

He beamed. "I did, actually. It was quite liberating. I made it to the golf course, but not inside the building."

"That's wonderful," I said. "The golf course is somewhere you used to spend a lot of time."

"Aye," Gareth agreed. "And I was able to watch a game. I must admit, it's a wee bit fun mocking the players when they can't hear you."

"I take it your friends weren't playing." Gareth's vampire friends tended to play golf at night.

"No, 'twas a group of werewolves. To be honest, I didn't realize they played golf. It seems far too civilized a sport for them. No disrespect intended."

"Well, I'm glad you enjoyed yourself. I hope your lucky streak continues. I would love it if you could show up at the Mayor's Mansion. That way if I don't attend, you can report back to me."

Gareth inclined his head. "You think you might not go?"

"I haven't decided yet. I think it might be too hard for me."

"Since when does Emma Hart shrink from a challenge? That's not the annoying and plucky roommate I know."

"Gee, thanks."

"Shouldn't you be ready to go by now?" Gareth asked.

I blinked. "I hardly think so. The party isn't today."

"Not the party. Markos. You mentioned having lunch with him today."

I smacked my forehead. "I almost forgot." I dashed into the bathroom and inspected my face in the mirror. "Zit City.

I need to make myself presentable before he gets here." I touched the angry pimple on my cheek. There had to be a spell to eliminate it.

"The time for miracles has long since passed," Gareth called from the bedroom.

"It's a miracle I put up with you," I shot back, just as the wind chimes sounded. "Crap on a stick."

Markos and I enjoyed a pleasant lunch at Toadstools. In truth, I was grateful for any meal that I didn't have to make. Cooking was not my forte, as Gareth liked to point out.

"How would you like a tour of the new headquarters?" Markos asked, as we returned to his jalopy. "You didn't exactly get the best impression last time."

"I would love that," I said. "Your designs are amazing. Everywhere I go in town, someone points out one of your masterpieces."

Markos seemed humbled by the praise. "The residents here have been very supportive of me. For that I am eternally grateful."

Markos was such a great guy. Everyone liked him and he seemed to like everyone in return. It was refreshing. I knew a guy like Markos in high school called Ron. Everyone called him the mayor, even the teachers. He seemed to unite people by the sheer force of his kind and effervescent personality. I wondered what Ron was doing now. I'd skipped my five-year reunion because I'd been buried in work at the time. I hadn't been disappointed to miss it because high school had been an okay experience. Not ideal but not terrible. I had to imagine Ron was in his element in social situations. A genuine extrovert.

"What's the latest with the case?" Markos asked. We

walked through the familiar lobby and I found myself admiring the endless ceiling all over again.

"Ha," I replied. "I was going to ask you the same question."

"I heard you've been working with Astrid."

"Only when her sister is unavailable," I said. I didn't want to mention the particulars of their difficult relationship. Astrid really wanted Britta to succeed as deputy, so we needed to give her time to get into the swing of things.

Markos grinned. "You've seen the lobby and the kitchen. Would you like to see my office this time?"

"Lead on," I said.

We took what appeared to be a freestanding elevator to the top floor. I studied the glass enclosure, trying to figure out how it operated. Markos noticed my interest.

"Pixie dust," he admitted sheepishly. "I didn't say that I don't use *any* magic in my buildings."

The doors opened and we stepped into an enormous room with wall-to-wall windows on all four sides that provided a panoramic view of the town. I ran to the nearest window to admire the scene below.

"Wow. What an amazing space. This whole floor is your office?"

"Mostly mine," he said. "Nellie is on this floor, too." He paused to listen. "In fact, she's here now."

"How do you know?"

"Because I can hear her talking to herself. She does it all the time."

"My grandfather was like that," I said. He talked to the television, talked to his crossword puzzles, talked to himself about where he'd left his glasses (usually on his head). "I guess Nellie isn't such a good listener if she's always talking, huh?"

Markos chuckled. "She's an excellent office manager, that's for sure. Come on, I'll introduce you."

We walked to the corner of the room where a small area was carved out for the office manager with a desk and several filing cabinets. The nymph glanced up from a document when we entered the room. "Oh, I didn't hear anyone come up."

Markos grinned at me. "You were saying?"

"You know I'm hard of hearing." Although Nellie glared at him, I could tell that it was good-natured and part of their dynamic.

"Nellie Granger, this is Emma Hart," Markos said.

Nellie looked me up and down. "Finally we meet. The gods know I have to hear your name often enough. I hope you said yes to the engagement party. Markos has been talking about it nonstop."

Markos held up a finger. "Ahem, Nellie."

Nellie froze. "Oh, you haven't asked her yet, have you? Oops."

Markos turned to me. "I was planning to ask you over lunch, but I got distracted."

"By what?" I asked.

Nellie gave a high-pitched laugh. "By you, of course."

I didn't know what to say. "I hadn't decided on my reply."

"There's no need," Markos said. "I told them I was bringing a guest. May as well be you, right?"

I hesitated. As much as it pained me, I hated to miss a special event in Daniel's life. With Markos by my side, it might be easier to cope.

"Okay," I said. "Let's go together. As friends, of course."

Markos beamed. "Of course."

"Thank the gods," Nellie said. "Now I can stop hearing about it."

I walked over to peer out of her window. "What's your view?"

"The parking lot," Nellie said tartly. "Only the best for the office manager."

"Now Nellie," Markos said. "You know if you bother to look beyond the parking lot, you can see all the way to Swan Lake."

"It's lovely," I said. "With a view like that, you must be inspired all day."

"Inspired to stab myself in the heart with this quill," Nellie replied. "These reports are a mess."

"Numbers don't match again?" Markos queried.

Nellie shook her head. "I'm trying to reconcile them, but it will take time."

"You can't reconcile what isn't there," Markos said. "At some point, we need to accept that there might be a problem."

Nellie placed her palms flat on the desk. "Leave it with me, boss. I'll get to the bottom of it."

He patted her on the back. "I know you will, Nellie." He motioned for me to follow. "Come on, Emma. I'll show you my view."

"I think we both know the view you're interested in," Nellie muttered under her breath.

I stifled a laugh. They reminded me of a nephew and his ornery aunt.

Markos's view was far more impressive. It was almost as expansive as the view from Curse Cliff. "I've always found a good view inspiring," I said.

"Me too," Markos agreed. "I do my best thinking when I'm staring out the window."

"Were you a daydreamer as a child?" I asked.

He shoved his hands into his pockets. "Still am."

I liked that he hadn't become older and cynical. Then again, he seemed to have Nellie for that.

"Anything else I can show you?" he asked, with a mischievous gleam in his eye.

"No thanks," I said quickly. "I need to get to my own, much smaller office. I haven't been there for days and I think Althea is ready to send a search party. Thank you for lunch. It was fun."

"It was, wasn't it?" He grinned. "Let me drive you."

"It's such a beautiful day," I said. "I think I'll walk."

CHAPTER 6

I OPENED the window in my office to let in the fresh air. The weather was a few degrees warmer than usual and the small office felt stuffy, especially compared with Markos's massive space. As if sensing a change in the Force, Althea burst into the room. She took one look at the open window and her snakes began hissing wildly.

"What do you think you're doing?" she asked frantically. "Are you trying to kill all the plants on the windowsill?"

"It's too hot in here," I said. "I would think these plants could use fresh air too."

"They get plenty of fresh air," she said testily. "What do you think I do every morning? We have a system. Don't ruin it."

"You do remember that this is *my* office?" I said.

She shot me a look that made her snakes quiver. "Are you trying to put a Gorgon in her place? Because I'll tell you right now, it won't end well for you."

I quickly realized the error of my ways. "I'm sorry, Althea. I didn't mean to mess up your system." In *my* office.

Althea glanced at the open window and relented. "Fine. It

is a little hot in here. I suppose I'll let you leave it open for a while." She glanced at the barrel of moonshine that she kept stored behind my desk. "If it's too hot in here, my moonshine won't ferment properly. I have to keep the environment just right."

I glanced over my shoulder at the oversized container. "How did this monstrosity get back in here? I thought we discussed this."

Althea shrugged. "I tested other spots and this is the best one. For whatever reason, it provides the most conducive environment."

Well, I wasn't about to put a Gorgon in her place twice in one day. After all, I valued my life.

"There's a new file on my desk," I said. "Am I to assume that means I have a new client?"

"Your powers of deduction are astounding," she said. "Yes, a young werelion by the name of Will Heath. He was arrested for possession of nightshade. It's all there in the file, as usual." She shot me a haughty look. "I know how to do my job."

"I never suggested otherwise." I winked at her and the snakes hissed in reply.

"I have your coffee on my desk. Shall I get it for you? Or is my system not to your liking, Your Highness?"

I groaned. "Stop whining and bring me the coffee. Please," I added quickly.

She broke into a smile. "I do enjoy giving you a hard time. It amuses me."

The door opened and a young man took a hesitant step inside. "Miss Hart?"

"You must be Will. Come on in."

Will looked surprisingly small in stature for a werelion, yet appropriately surly given his age and circumstances. He was no taller than five feet, six inches with a slight build and shaggy brown hair. I wondered whether he was related to

Fabio, the werelion I'd had a single date with. My exposure to Curse Cliff had sent him into a tizzy and he'd quickly banned me from his list of eligible young women. It was no great disappointment since I'd only gone on the date in exchange for a favor from Pandora, the town matchmaker.

"So Will, it says here you were arrested in Mix-n-Match for possession of nightshade. Is that true?"

Will seemed to look everywhere in the room except at me. He mumbled a response.

"I'm sorry, Will, but I don't speak mumblese. Could you try and articulate for me?" Despite my curt tone, I wanted to cut him some slack. According to the file, he was only twenty years old.

"I said it's true," he said, still refusing to meet my gaze. "I had nightshade in my pocket."

"How did anyone know? Did you take it out to show someone?"

"No, I went to take coins out of my pocket to pay for a potion and the nightshade fell onto the floor. The shop-keeper recognized it and called Sheriff Astrid."

"Where did you get the nightshade? Did you buy it from someone?"

He slumped further in his chair. This time he focused on his shoes. "Does it matter? What's the worst option here? Prison time?"

I steepled my fingers together. "As a matter of fact, yes. Possession of nightshade can land you in Spellbound Prison for up to five years. You're a werelion at the height of your youth. I doubt that's where you want to spend the time."

"It's better than some people get," he said vaguely.

I studied him closely. "The minimum sentence is one year of community service. Obviously, that's what I'll try to get for you. I have a feeling if you reveal the source of the night-shade that the prosecution would be willing to bend."

This time he looked directly at me. "And what if I don't talk? Is the five-year sentence a guarantee?"

"No, of course not. It would just make the case easier. That's all." I had the distinct impression that Will was withholding information. "Will, what are you not telling me? I'm your lawyer. That means I'm on your side. If I'm to defend you to the best of my ability, it would be helpful to know everything. If you're protecting someone, like maybe the person who's growing the nightshade, then we'll figure out the best way to handle it."

He swallowed hard. "I'm not protecting the person who grows the nightshade." He shifted uncomfortably in his seat. "The truth is that I stole it, okay? I went into someone's garden in the middle of the night and clipped the nightshade."

"Why? What did you intend to do with it?" Nightshade was a deadly plant, far too dangerous for this young werelion to handle.

"Does it matter? Whatever it is, I won't be doing it now, will I?"

"Because Sheriff Astrid took the nightshade?"

He nodded. "And I don't want anyone to try and charge me with intent to commit another crime, do I?"

The young werelion wasn't stupid. That was a good thing for me.

"Where did you steal the nightshade from?"

"I don't remember," he said. His body language screamed deception.

"So you were just walking along in the middle of the night and stumbled upon some nightshade? Do you at least remember which part of town you were in?"

"I was in my lion form running along the countryside," he said. "I didn't really pay attention to exactly where I was."

"You said you clipped it from a garden," I reminded him.

"Was this in your lion form or when you changed back into human form?"

His eyes darted around the room. "I bit it off in my lion form. That's what I meant when I said I clipped it. I carried it back in my mouth."

A likely story. Now I was certain Will was hiding something and it was up to me to figure out what it was.

"I appreciate you coming in, Will. I hope you don't mind the sight of me because I have a feeling we're going to be seeing a lot of each other over the next couple of weeks. If you stop by Althea's desk on your way out, she'll schedule your next appointment."

He mumbled a response and rose to his feet.

"What was that?" I asked. "If this case goes to trial, Will, we're going to have to figure out a way to keep you from mumbling."

He turned back to look at me. "I said I don't mind the sight of you." With those clear and concise words, he continued into Althea's office.

Hmm. Maybe not such a surly werelion after all.

Lady Weatherby stood at the head of the classroom, wand in hand. "Today we will be mastering..." She cleared her throat. "I beg your pardon. Today we will be *experimenting* with a Weaken spell. Like many other spells we've learned, this spell is intended to be used defensively. For example, if you have an opponent who is physically stronger than you, use the spell to weaken and overpower them."

Millie raised her hand.

I noticed the subtle eye roll before Lady Weatherby said, "Yes, Millie?"

"How do we know if our opponent is physically stronger than us? I mean, obviously if it's a minotaur or something, that's obvious, but what about someone like another witch?"

Naturally she had to choose a minotaur as her example. Since Markos was the only minotaur in town, I had no doubt it was a dig at me. Millie couldn't seem to help herself. If she wasn't careful, she was going to turn into the next Jemima. I don't think any of the remedial witches wanted to see that transformation.

"If you're uncertain, then perhaps you would consider using a different spell," Lady Weatherby said. "As you know, Millie, there are many other defensive spells at your disposal. Choose the one that best suits the situation."

Millie's cheeks reddened. The response was a smack-down, subtle though it was.

"Now I am in need of two volunteers," Lady Weatherby said.

Millie's hand shot up again and Lady Weatherby nodded for her to speak. "Shouldn't it be the smallest and biggest in the class? That way one is clearly stronger than the other."

Lady Weatherby's lips formed a thin line. "For our purposes today, it doesn't matter whether one is, in fact, stronger than the other. The spell will work either way." She paused and gave her a pointed look. "As long as you perform it correctly, that is."

Millie sank into her chair. I had a feeling she would not be volunteering today.

Sophie raised her hand. "I volunteer."

"Very well then, Sophie. Come to the front, please."

Sophie pushed back her chair and moved to stand at the head of the class.

"One more, please," Lady Weatherby said. When no one volunteered, Lady Weatherby lifted a sculpted dark eyebrow. "Surely you can't think Sophie will harm anyone with the spell."

No one responded. Sophie was known for her spells backfiring. She was always a trooper, though—always willing to volunteer despite her inadequacies. I felt my hand slide into the air. I couldn't bear to leave her alone up there.

"Very well, Miss Hart," Lady Weatherby said. "To the front. We don't have all day."

I joined Sophie at the front of the classroom and we stood about four feet apart.

"I shall demonstrate first, and then you will each have a turn." Lady Weatherby pointed her wand at Sophie and said, "A hive of honeybees/weak in the knees."

Sophie crumpled to the ground as though her legs were too weak to support her body. She remained sprawled on the floor for a good two minutes before dragging herself back to her feet.

"The effects of the spell last for about two minutes," Lady Weatherby explained.

Millie's hand waved in the air. "Just enough time to get away."

"Thank you, Millie," Lady Weatherby said. "Like other defensive spells, it is generally meant to give you time to escape and get help."

The Weaken spell would've come in handy a few times for me already. It was a shame I didn't know more spells.

"Sophie, why don't you try the spell on Emma, if you're feeling back to full strength," Lady Weatherby said.

Sophie smiled. "Back to full strength, ma'am." She scrunched her face in concentration and stared at me. Then she extended her wand and said, "Feel the breeze/weak in the knees."

Nothing happened. I'd been mentally prepared to fall to the ground, but there I stood, feeling…better. I glanced nervously over my shoulder at Lady Weatherby.

Sophie shot me a helpless look. "Nothing?"

I shook my head.

"Sometimes the spell impacts a different part of the body," Lady Weatherby said. "Perhaps her legs did not weaken, but her arms did."

That seemed plausible. "Why don't you see if you can overpower me?" I asked. "Then we'll know."

"Good idea," Lady Weatherby said. My knees nearly buckled at the compliment. Who needed a spell?

Sophie cautiously approached me. "How do I overpower you? I don't want to hit you."

"Maybe try to wrestle me to the ground?" We were fairly evenly matched physically—similar height and weight. I had an inch and a few extra years on her, but that was all.

Sophie grabbed me by the arms and tried to push me to the ground. Instinctively, I pushed back. Sophie went flying across the room and landed straight in the basket of drop cloths used during advanced mixology. She groaned and dragged herself to a standing position.

I rushed toward her, horrified. "Sophie, I'm so sorry. I don't understand what happened."

"It's okay," she said. "I'm not hurt."

"Thank the stars," Millie said.

"Can anyone tell the class what went wrong?" Lady Weatherby asked, unperturbed.

Laurel raised her hand. "She held the wrong end of the wand?"

It wouldn't be the first time that happened. Sophie and I returned to our places in front of the class.

"Not this time, Laurel," Lady Weatherby said. "Anyone else?"

Sophie's hand rose. She wore a guilty expression. "I didn't focus my will."

Lady Weatherby seemed pleased that she'd figured it out. "No?"

"No," Sophie confirmed. "As I was saying the spell, I was actually thinking how strong Emma was. I didn't mean physically, more like strength of character."

Millie snorted. "I guess you won't be having that thought again."

Lady Weatherby silenced Millie with a sharp look. "Well done, Sophie. Although I would prefer that you get spells correct on the first try, it is equally important that we are able to identify and correct our own mistakes. It is a useful skill in the classroom as well as in life."

"Can I try again?" Sophie asked.

"I insist upon it," Lady Weatherby said.

Sophie focused on me and extended her wand. "These words I speak/make her weak."

My body suddenly felt like it was made of jelly. I could hardly move a muscle. Even my mouth seemed too tired to form words. "I…" Yep, too weak to speak. I knew a few people I'd like to try this spell on.

"Did it work?" Sophie asked hopefully.

"I think you'll find it did," Lady Weatherby said. "Well done, Sophie."

Sophie beamed like she'd been awarded a gold star.

"I believe it's Emma turn," Millie said.

Lady Weatherby nodded toward me. I focused my will and pointed my wand at Sophie. "Power I seek/make her weak."

Sophie didn't simply crumple to the floor this time. She dropped straight down like a sack of bricks.

I smiled proudly at Lady Weatherby. "I did it."

"Um, Lady Weatherby," Laurel said. "Sophie doesn't seem to be moving. At all."

Lady Weatherby glanced down. "Sophie?"

The pile of skin and bones formerly known as Sophie

made no reply. I rushed forward and dropped to my knees. I rolled her onto her back to see that her eyes were closed.

"I don't think she's breathing," I said.

Lady Weatherby was at my side in a heartbeat. "Give me room to work, please," she said, reaching for her wand.

I backed away and watched as she touched the wand to Sophie's forehead. The tip of the wand glowed like the color of the sun. When Sophie stirred, my stomach unclenched.

"Sophie, are you with us?" Lady Weatherby asked. There was no trace of panic in her voice. I, on the other hand, had nothing but panic racing through my veins. I didn't think it was possible to be as calm and cool as Lady Weatherby.

Sophie's eyelids fluttered open. "Did it work?"

Everybody laughed.

"The spell wasn't meant to make her unconscious," Millie said. "Would you really say that it worked?"

"The point is to weaken your opponent," Lady Weatherby said. "If, for you, that means rendering the other person unconscious, then so be it. I consider it a success, however excessive."

A success? It didn't feel like a success. I nearly killed my friend. That was nothing but a monumental failure in my book.

"I wasn't trying to make her unconscious, though," I said. "Not even when I focused my will."

Lady Weatherby studied me. "I see. Miss Hart, why don't you see me after class?"

Talk about a Weaken spell. My body went limp. "Yes, ma'am," I croaked.

I sat in the chair across from Lady Weatherby's desk, admiring the portrait of Arabella St. Simon, the academy's namesake. She looked just as grand as I remembered from my last visit.

"Professor Holmes," Lady Weatherby said. "Thank you for joining us last minute."

Professor Holmes dropped into the chair next to me. "Emma again?"

""We had a bit of an incident in class today," Lady Weatherby explained. "It seems our own Miss Hart packs a more powerful magical punch than the other remedial witches."

"Not really," I protested.

Chairman Meow came out from behind the desk to hiss at me, as though arguing on his familiar's behalf. His little antler headdress was slightly askew, making him look more adorable then he probably would have liked.

"We were performing a simple Weaken spell, but Miss Hart seems to have rendered our young Sophie unconscious in the process."

Professor Holmes cast a sidelong glance at me. "Is that so? And was that your intention?"

"Of course not," I blurted. "Sophie's one of my best friends. I would never want to hurt her."

"I wasn't suggesting that you would," Professor Holmes said. "I'm sorry. I know you're very fond of Sophie."

"I'm fond of all of them, even Millie." As soon as the words were out of my mouth, I longed to snatch them back. To my relief, both Professor Holmes and Lady Weatherby chuckled.

"Millie has a good heart," Professor Holmes said.

"She can, however, ruffle even the most docile of feathers," Lady Weatherby said.

"She's jealous of you, you know," Professor Holmes said.

"I don't see why she would be," I said. "Everyone knows she's the star pupil of the class."

"Yes, and, despite that, you came from nowhere and

easily made the friends that it has taken her years to culti-vate," Professor Holmes said. "Her personality is more abra-sive than yours. It takes longer for people to warm up to her."

"Well, we have had our differences," I admitted. Her jeal-ousy had reared its head early on, when she cursed me with a spell that made my boobs the size of watermelons. We'd talked it through at the time and made up. I felt confident that we were in a better place now.

"When you focused your will," Lady Weatherby began, "what exactly were you thinking?"

I closed my eyes, trying to remember my exact thoughts. "I was hoping that she dropped to the floor in the same way she did when you performed the spell. I wanted the effect of the spell to be obvious, so that there was no question of my success."

"Mmm," Lady Weatherby said. "You achieved your goal. There was certainly no question about that."

"Am I in trouble?" I asked.

"Not today," Lady Weatherby said. "But try to keep your will as specific as possible and remember your strength. Apparently, it isn't limited to your character." She gave me a wry smile.

"That strength might come in handy tomorrow night," Professor Holmes said cryptically.

"What's tomorrow…?" Then I remembered. The engage-ment party. Spell's bells—did everyone in town know about my feelings for Daniel? "Will you be there?"

"We will," Lady Weatherby said. "We expect to see you on your best behavior." Translation: no magic to mess up the party.

"Of course, Lady Weatherby," I said.

The problem with being on my best behavior was that it always ended with me holding the losing end of the stick. I sighed inwardly. I had no doubt that tomorrow evening would be no different.

I was polishing my notes from my meeting with Will when a knock on the office door took me by surprise. I rarely had drop-ins.

"Althea," I called. "Do I have a client meeting?" It wouldn't be the first time that I was given short notice.

She poked her head in the doorway, the snakes bumping and grinding beneath her turban. "No, do you want me to answer it?"

"I can hear you both," a muffled voice said. "It's Astrid."

"Oh. Well, come in," I yelled.

The door opened and the blond Valkyrie appeared. "I guess it was silly to knock."

I gestured her forward. "You're the sheriff now. You can walk in any place you like."

She puffed out her chest. "I am the sheriff, aren't I?"

"How are you finding it? Harder than you thought?"

She took a seat. "In some ways, yes. Mostly no. We both know Sheriff Hugo wasn't pulling his weight for years. It feels good to finally just step in and be in charge."

I could understand that. "And how's Britta getting on as deputy?"

"It's gotten better. Thanks for stepping in," she said. "I thought we would bicker more, but we seem to be working well together. For now, anyway."

"That's great news," I said. "What brings you here today?"

"I understand you met with Will Heath," she said. "Did he happen to mention where he obtained the nightshade?"

I tilted my head. "Astrid, you know I can't tell you that. Client confidentiality."

Astrid blew out a breath. "I figured, but I'm concerned

someone is selling nightshade on the side. We can't have a black market for poisonous plants in Spellbound."

"I will tell you that whatever the answer is, he hasn't given it to me yet. If it's something I think you should know, then I'll find a way to share the information." Even if that meant getting my client's permission.

Her blue eyes fixed on me. "I think it must be Janis Goodfellow, don't you? She's that witch who was determined to grow nightshade in her garden despite the ordinances."

I'd met Janis Goodfellow recently, when I was investigating a different case. She certainly didn't strike me as the type of person to seek a profit from poisonous plants.

"Have you gone to see Janis?" I asked.

Astrid shook her head. "Not yet. I was hoping you would get something out of Will."

"You know what? How about I go and speak to her? I'd like to know if she provided the nightshade to Will since he isn't talking. Let me speak to her as part of my case."

Astrid considered it for a moment. "Okay," she agreed. "I trust your judgment, Emma."

"How is the investigation going into Ed's death?" I asked. "I imagine that's keeping you busy."

Astrid rolled her eyes. "You have no idea. There's no telling when someone tampered with the ladder."

"What about Ed's enemies? Have you looked into the reasons anyone would want him dead? The notebooks we found in his house seemed to mention a few disgruntled people."

"They've been useful. We're speaking with more owners of buildings that didn't pass inspection," Astrid said. She gave me a curious look. "We'll be speaking to Markos in more depth."

My brow lifted. "Why? Because Ed was found in his building?"

Astrid nodded. "And there were rumors that Ed wasn't going to pass the building. It required some remediation."

"I hardly think that makes the case for murder," I said. "Especially considering Markos is a pretty well-known architect and an all-around nice minotaur."

Astrid shrugged. "You know how this goes. We have to follow up every lead."

I understood. I'd be the same, wanting to tug every thread and see what unraveled.

"Should I be there when you talk to him?" I asked.

Astrid narrowed her eyes. "Why? Are you thinking he might need a lawyer?"

"No, but he might need a friend." And I was certainly that.

"I don't mind if you're there. You always seem to have good insight."

I smiled. "I love the idea of working *with* each other instead of against each other." That certainly wasn't my experience with Sheriff Hugo.

She wiggled her eyebrows. "That's because there's a new sheriff in town."

Astrid was new and she still had to prove herself. "You know what? I think I'll skip your official talk with Markos. People might think you're giving him special treatment. I don't want my presence to undermine your good work."

"Suit yourself. Are we on for poker next week?"

"That's a great idea," I said. "I'll invite your sister too."

"She'd like that," Astrid said. "She's been complaining for weeks about not being included in anything."

"I'll have Sedgwick send out the invites tonight," I said.

Astrid hesitated before standing. "Speaking of invites, I suppose you received yours."

I sighed. "As a matter fact I did. A little over the top."

"Yes, but I wouldn't expect anything less from Elsa

Knightsbridge. She is nothing if not over the top. How are you feeling?"

"I'm not feeling," I said. "At least I'm trying not to feel anything at all. After all, you can't lose what was never yours."

Astrid gave me a sympathetic look. "If it's any consolation, I'm still rooting for you."

"Thanks, Astrid. You're a good friend."

"Right back at you," she said, and left the office.

CHAPTER 7

THE THEME of the engagement party seemed to be 'Wishes Do Come True.' The Cinderella-style carriage that delivered the invitations sat on display in front of the mansion, driving the point home. Inside the grand foyer was a fountain filled with pink, sparkling hearts. I walked over to investigate.

"They look liquid," I said, reaching down to swirl around the hearts.

Beside me, Markos smiled. "You know Mayor Knightsbridge. She spares no expense."

"As long as it's not taxpayer money she's spending, I have no problem with it." Okay, in truth I had a huge problem with it, but it had nothing to do with how she spent her money. It was the fact that she was celebrating her daughter's engagement to the fallen angel whom she loathed. Although I didn't know what Mayor Knightsbridge had planned, I knew this entire affair was a ruse. She had no intention of allowing her precious daughter to marry Daniel. Not after he'd humiliated the family the first time around.

A fairy footman ushered us into the ballroom where the

fairytale theme continued. It reminded me of the 'Be Our Guest' scene in *Beauty and the Beast*. The entire room appeared to be enchanted. There were spinning plates and dancing cutlery. Guests clapped as food appeared on their plates. Everyone in town seemed to be in attendance. I spotted Lady Weatherby and Professor Holmes chatting at a table. Instead of centerpieces, each table had a mini butterfly tempest. They created enough color and movement to be beautiful without being too distracting. I wondered what type of spell kept the butterflies from breaking formation.

"I see the happy couple on the dance floor," Markos said.

I almost didn't want to look. The last time I'd seen Daniel on the dance floor, I had been the one in his arms. It was where we'd exchanged our first and only kiss. Even though our flirtation had been an act that evening (on his end, at least), the kiss had felt deliciously real. So real, in fact, that I was sure that I'd seen a reaction in his turquoise eyes.

"They make a handsome couple, don't they?" Marisol Minor stood beside me in her human form.

"No one can argue with that," Markos said.

Marisol eyed us appreciatively. "You two make rather a nice couple as well," she said.

"That's very kind of you to say," I said. "But we're not a couple."

"Maybe not today, but there's always tomorrow. Take it from me. You don't want to waste your youth." She ambled off into the crowd, clutching an empty glass of wine.

A server came by with a tray of flutes. "Bucksberry fizz?"

"It looks like champagne," I said.

Markos plucked two flutes from the tray and handed one to me. "Similar, but a hint more sweetness."

I took a sip, allowing the bubbles to tickle my nose. "It's very good." I wasn't a huge fan of champagne, but Bucksberry fizz had just the right amount of sweet and tart.

"Good to see you, Markos," a familiar voice said. I turned to see the centaur formerly known as Sheriff Hugo. To be honest, I was surprised to see him in attendance. He and Mayor Knightsbridge had been close friends until her recent decision to remove him from his law enforcement position. She'd been counting on him to find the resident responsible for casting the youth spell on the town council, but, as usual, he'd been more interested in improving his golf handicap. Now he had all the time in the world to play.

Markos clapped the centaur on the back. "How are you holding up, Hugo? Keeping yourself busy?"

"I've improved my golf game, so that's a plus," he said.

I resisted the urge to roll my eyes.

Hugo shot me a look of annoyance out of the corner of his eye before fixing his attention on Markos. "I heard you had a bit of trouble at your new office."

"Poor Ed," Markos said. "I hope Sheriff Astrid is able to get to the bottom of it quickly. I don't want my employees to think there's a murderer running around the office. It's bad for morale."

"Well, let me know if you need a private consultant on the case," Hugo said. "I'm happy to offer my expertise if you find the current sheriff lacking."

I stifled an objection. Astrid was doing a fine job. In fact, Astrid had been doing his job long before she was given the title. Sheriff Hugo was nothing more than a lazy, good-for-nothing layabout.

"Thanks, Hugo. I'll keep that in mind." Markos turned toward me. "Is it too early to dance? Do you need another drink first?"

I laughed. "Liquid courage?"

"You look a bit nervous," he said. "I thought maybe a dance would help you loosen up."

I glanced at the dance floor where Daniel and Elsa were

still entwined in each other's arms. Somehow, I didn't think a turn on the dance floor was going to help my nerves.

"Maybe later," I said. "There are so many people here. I feel like we should mingle more."

"As you wish." He offered me his arm and together we moved around the ballroom, stopping to chat with guests we knew. His behavior reminded me of his party, the one he didn't know I'd attended. I'd been turned invisible by a wizard and had decided to check out the party anyway. I'd watched Markos greet his guests and he'd impressed me with his ability to work a room. It wasn't in a seedy political way either. His intentions were genuine. He seemed to enjoy talking to the guests. No wonder he was so popular. It was a far cry from Daniel, who seemed to inspire lust and derision in equal measure.

"Miss Hart. You are a vision this evening."

"Lord Gilder." I greeted the head of the vampire coven. "It's nice to see you."

Lord Gilder nodded at Markos. "You've chosen wisely this evening, Markos. Not that I would expect anything less from you."

Markos chuckled. "I was happy she chose to say yes."

Lord Gilder's thin lips formed a smile. "Yes, she is proving herself rather resourceful." He focused on me. "And how is our mutual friend?"

I knew he was referring to Gareth. Word had gotten around about my vampire ghost roommate.

"He's doing better every day," I said. "He was hoping to make an appearance here tonight, but his skills aren't quite there yet."

"Well, I do hope you will let me know when they are," Lord Gilder said. "Or invite me to the next séance. I would very much like to say hello to my old friend."

"Absolutely. Gareth would love that." It was true. Gareth

had a lot of respect for his former leader. He still spoke very highly of Lord Gilder.

"Oh, look," I said, pointing to the bar where Dr. Hall was watching us like a hungry hawk. "There's my therapist." I waved and she immediately turned away and snapped her fingers for another drink.

Lord Gilder glanced over his shoulder. "Ah, Catherine. How nice for you. She's a real treat. A bit unorthodox, as I understand it."

"You could say that," I agreed.

"There you are. I've been looking everywhere for you." Lucy drifted toward me, her pink wings flapping wildly. "I love this dress. You look divine."

I admired her flapper-style dress with its intricate bead-work. "Same to you. Did you end up bringing a date?" Lucy had debated for days whether to attend alone because she figured that the mayor would end up putting her to work at some point during the evening.

"I decided against it," she said. "Duty calls and all that."

As if on cue, Mayor Knightsbridge appeared beside Lucy. "Darling, I thought I asked you to refill the chocolate river. The current has slowed considerably."

"Yes, Mayor Knightsbridge. I asked the caterers to take care of it only a minute ago."

Mayor Knightsbridge shifted her focus to me. "Emma, thank you so much for coming." She looked at Markos. "And with one of the most delectable bachelors in town. Well done, you." It was no surprise that her smile failed to reach her eyes. Mayor Knightsbridge was counting on me to help break up the union between Elsa and Daniel. She knew very well what my real feelings for him were and she was intent on using them to her advantage. I was sure the sight of me with Markos made her anxious.

"Well done to me," Markos said, placing an arm along my

67

shoulders. "I feel quite fortunate to have made a friend like Emma."

"Too right, Markos," Mayor Knightsbridge said. "It's lovely to see you both here. Emma, have you managed to say hello to the guests of honor yet?"

My gaze automatically drifted to the celebrated couple, still on the dance floor. "Not yet. We're slowly making our way there."

"Don't wait too long," the mayor said. "Time to mingle. I'll see you all later." She fluttered into the crowd, blowing kisses like she was the queen.

"They'll be leaving the dance floor shortly," Lucy said. "The next phase of entertainment will be starting."

The next phase of entertainment? I wondered what that could be. I didn't have a chance to ask because Daniel appeared behind Lucy, surprising us.

"Emma, you're here," Daniel said. "I thought you didn't RSVP." He looked so happy to see me that my heart squeezed.

"I'm here," I said. And was regretting every second of it now. "Daniel, you know my date, Markos."

Daniel glanced at Markos and I was almost certain I saw him flinch. "Of course. Thank you for coming. Elsa and I are so pleased with the turnout."

"She's a beautiful fairy," Markos said. "I hope you two will be very happy together."

It didn't escape my notice that everyone who mentioned Elsa's good qualities only seemed to focus on her beauty. No one ever remarked on her kindness or her dazzling personality. It spoke volumes. Once again, I found myself wondering what on earth had sparked Daniel's change of heart.

Before I could say another word, Elsa joined her fiancé. She draped herself on his arm like she was a third appendage. It took all of my will not to bust out my wand and turn her into a toad. Lady Weatherby's warning rang in my head. She seemed to know me better than I knew myself.

"Emma Hart. Daniel's little friend. Am I to understand that you're here with our beloved Markos?" She gave us both a dazzling smile. "Daniel, honey, did you know that Emma and Markos were an item?"

"Not an item," Markos said. "Just here as friends."

"Still, they make a very attractive couple, don't they?" Elsa looked expectantly at her betrothed and I wanted to vomit.

Daniel forced a smile. "Emma looks lovely, as always. Like Markos said, though, they're not a couple. Emma would have told me."

The way you told me about your engagement to Elsa? I wanted to shout. I hated that I had to hear the news from someone else. Daniel was supposed to be my best friend, but he only came to me after half the town knew about it. I didn't want to cause a scene over it now, though. Water under the bridge.

"I'm sorry to interrupt," Lucy said. "It's time for photographs. Miranda is waiting in the foyer." Miranda was the eldest of the three Gorgon sisters and a professional photographer. It didn't surprise me that she'd been hired to photograph the event.

"Come along, honey," Elsa said, dragging Daniel by the hand.

Daniel resisted slightly and I noticed Elsa frown. "You know what? I think we should grab a quick drink before we have our photos taken."

"I can grab you both drinks," Lucy offered. Elsa waved her off.

"I know what Daniel likes," she said. "I like to be the one to take care of my man."

Lucy shrugged. "I'd hurry if I were you. It's never a good idea to keep a Gorgon waiting."

Amen to that. Nobody wanted to piss off Althea. Her stare might not turn you to stone anymore, but it might make you pee your pants.

Markos waited until they were out of earshot to speak. "Well, I guess it's nice to see her doting on him. She's normally so self-centered."

Lucy's laugh tinkled. "It's funny, isn't it? Most of the time, she's the same old Elsa. Making demands. Bossing him around. With certain things, though, she's adamant about doing it for him. Sometimes I expect her to cut his meat for him. It's bizarre."

"He still seems smitten," I said. It was hard to keep the disappointment out of my voice.

Markos cast a sidelong glance at me. "He's a fool, Emma. Plain and simple. I must admit, though, that I hope his loss might eventually be my gain." He gave me a look that left me in no doubt as to what his true intentions were.

"I'm flattered, Markos," I said. "But I meant what I said before. I'm not in a place in my life where a relationship makes any sense. There's too much on my plate right now. I mean it about wanting to be friends, though. I can never have too many friends in Spellbound."

He extended a hand. "Can friends dance together in your world?"

I accepted his hand. "Absolutely."

Together we made our way to the dance floor. He moved just as well as the night I'd seen him dance at his own party. He was a natural, unlike me. I managed to bumble my way through the next few songs, praying that I didn't knock anyone over. At least Markos was tall and solidly built. There was little chance of me injuring him.

A slow song began and he pulled me gently into his arms. He was so tall that I had to crane my neck to see his face.

"I'm sure it isn't easy for you," Markos said, gazing into my eyes. "But I'm glad you came."

"Me too," I said, and I hoped by the end of the evening that I actually meant it.

CHAPTER 8

I WAS RELIEVED the next day when Gareth reminded me that I had another appointment with Dr. Catherine Hall. As strange as she was, I needed someone to vent to after the engagement party, even if I only ended up complaining about the weather.

I sat down on the red velvet wingback chair and Catherine handed me a glass of her other favorite drink, Arrogant Bitch.

"Are you sure we shouldn't be having herbal tea or something?" I asked. Tea seemed much more appropriate in a therapist's office.

"Tea is for weaklings who can't handle their liquor," Catherine said dismissively. She narrowed her eyes. "You're not one of those, are you? If you are, we might need to rethink our relationship."

"We need to rethink our therapist-client relationship because I don't want to drink hard alcohol in the middle of the day?" Someone's priorities were out of order and it wasn't me.

"Listen, I've been around for a lot longer than you. Trust

me when I tell you that people are always more interesting when they've had a little alcohol in their system."

"But I'm not trying to be interesting," I countered. "I'm trying to get therapy."

Catherine rolled her eyes. "Then what's in it for me if you're not interesting? I don't do this job for the money."

She certainly had an interesting attitude toward her role as a therapist. I decided to roll with it.

"Is Thalia of a similar mindset?" I asked.

Catherine sucked down more of her drink. "That precious flower? Are you kidding me? She's about as entertaining as a fly on a unicorn's butt. It boggles the brain that people want to confess anything to her."

"Well, I'm not really confessing anything," I said. "We're just talking. I'm supposed to tell you how I feel." I hesitated. "That's how therapy is supposed to work, right?"

Catherine rolled her hand in an effort to say 'yes, yes, get on with it.' "What is it that you'd like to talk about today?"

"Althea thinks it will be helpful if I talk about my mother's death," I said, fidgeting. It wasn't an easy topic for me. "She thinks I keep a lot of things bottled up and that it prevents me from expressing my feelings."

Catherine nibbled on a piece of ice. "Who doesn't? We're all powder kegs on the verge of explosion. Okay then, tell me the story. How did she die?"

"She drowned when I was three," I said. I felt the knots forming in my body as I spoke. "It was hard for a few years after that. My father didn't cope very well at first. It forced me to grow up fast. To take care of both of us." Catherine choked back laughter and I stiffened in my chair. "I'm sorry. Did I say something funny?"

"Yes, your mother drowned when you were little. That's very sad." She pretended to wipe a fictitious tear from her eye. "I can do you one better. Try coping when both of your parents drown at the same time."

My eyes widened. "Both your parents drowned?" I immediately felt terrible for raising the subject.

"We were traveling by ship to America from Liverpool, back when crossing the ocean was the only way to get anywhere. The ship was attacked by a Kraken. We lost half the crew and a third of the passengers, including my parents."

"A Kraken? I thought those were make-believe."

"Says the young witch in therapy with a vampire."

Good point. "How old were you?"

"Ten," she said, showing no emotion whatsoever. "I left Liverpool with a family and arrived in New York as an orphan."

I sucked in a breath. "Wow. Makes my experience sound so tame."

"I know. Right?" She wiggled her fingers. "What else have you got for me?"

I wanted to talk more about her experience. What happened to her after that? She obviously became a vampire later in life. How did she cope all of those years? Who raised her? I could tell by her stony expression that my inquiries would get me nowhere.

"Do you ever talk about your experience?" I prodded.

"All the time," she said. "It's part of my approach to therapy. You tell me what happened to you and I tell you how it could've been worse."

So her style was competitive vampire therapist. At least I knew early on what to expect.

"Did you like your mother?" Catherine asked.

"I loved her with all of my heart," I said, bringing my knees to my chest. "She gave the best hugs in the world. And she gave me my stuffed owl, Huey. I treasured him."

Until the day I arrived in Spellbound and left him behind forever.

"Why did you love her? How did she make you feel special?" She tapped her nails impatiently on the side of her glass, making a hollow, clicking sound.

"I don't have a lot of specific memories," I said. "More like bits and pieces of a puzzle. Images will flash in my mind. Or I'll smell something that reminds me of her."

"My mother told me every day that I was the most beautiful girl in the world," Catherine said. "She told me there wasn't a person of the world who wouldn't love me because I was so wonderful. She smelled like rainbows and unicorns."

I nearly laughed, except I got the distinct impression that she was serious. "I don't know what unicorns and rainbows smell like."

She shook her head sadly. "That's a shame. You should go to the pasture one of these days and find yourself a unicorn. You haven't really experienced life until you see one up close."

"Is there a special pasture where they hang out?" I would definitely put that at the top of my list.

"I would try near Curse Cliff. Whenever I need to be reminded of my mother, I drive over there and find one to rub its horn." She shrugged. "It's good luck."

I made a mental note. It was hard to believe I hadn't seen one yet.

"You said your father fell apart after your mother's death," Catherine said. "What sorts of things did he do?"

"At the time, I thought he was very sad. Now that I'm older, I see that he was severely depressed. He couldn't get out of bed. He couldn't do daily tasks without great effort, if at all. I learned how to take care of him and the house."

"That's nothing," Catherine said. "After my parents died, I stopped talking for two years. I was a selective mute. People in America didn't know I could talk until one day I opened my mouth and sound came out again."

"That's incredible," I said. "What made you start talking again?"

"I don't remember. I just did." She inclined her head. "You're not crying."

I touched my face self-consciously. "Do you want me to cry? Is that a requirement?"

"No, I have no tolerance for crybabies. Quite the opposite in fact. Crying gets in the way of good conversation."

I'd have to bear that in mind.

"You seem to have managed rather well in life," she said. "Are you sure you've been impacted by your parents' death?"

What kind of question was that? "I don't think there's an orphan on earth who could possibly say that they weren't negatively impacted by the death of their parents."

Catherine shrugged. "I guess so. Still, you did well in school. You went to law school. You obviously found a way to do more than survive."

"Maybe. I'm not very good with relationships, though. Or at least I haven't been until I came here."

Catherine polished off the rest of her drink and set the glass on the coffee table. "What do you think is different about here? Other than the obvious addition of horns and wings."

I examined my nails, thinking. "I don't know. Maybe because Spellbound is so different that I've been focused on things other than my emotional baggage."

"So you've made friends, but you still didn't manage to confess your feelings to Daniel before he chose someone else. That's gotta sting, right?"

For a therapist, she wasn't very sensitive. "This again?"

"This again. I mean, the party was last night. You went. How was it?"

"Hard," I admitted.

"Why didn't you tell him last night? It would've been quite the story around town."

I gasped. "I couldn't do that last night."

"Apparently you couldn't do it any night."

I sighed. "You're right. As much as I wanted to, I couldn't manage it. I was afraid that he wouldn't return my feelings and I'd lose him forever, the way I lost my parents."

"But you didn't lose your parents because you loved them," Catherine pointed out. It was the most sensible thing she'd said yet.

"We've become such good friends," I explained. "I rely on him for support and enjoy his company so much that I couldn't risk making things awkward between us."

"Well, mission not accomplished. He's engaged to someone else. Things will certainly be awkward now." She leaned forward and patted me on the shoulder. "Good job, Emma."

I shook her off. "Okay, no need to be mean about it."

"You think you've got it bad," she said. "Let me tell you my horrific love story. His name was Liam."

"Human or vampire?" I asked.

"I was a vampire. He was a vampire slayer. You can see the problem already, can't you?"

"I'm sorry, Catherine. That's so tragic." It was like a vampire Romeo and Juliet, except Romeo wasn't trained to hunt and kill Juliet.

"He used a special sword to send me to a hell dimension. Later a witch's spell resurrected me. And here I am."

Her story sounded oddly familiar. Then it hit me. "Catherine, you're making this up. That's the plot of season two of *Buffy the Vampire Slayer*." Only the genders were reversed.

Catherine bit back a smile. "Damnation. I forget you

came from the human world. I may have ways of tapping into your entertainment."

It didn't surprise me. If the remedial witches had access to movies and television, I had to imagine that other supernaturals in town did as well.

"So have you ever been in love?" I asked.

Catherine nodded toward the glass in my hand. "You haven't finished your drink."

It didn't escape my notice that she changed the subject. There was a story there. I knew it. The sound of screeching bats interrupted us and I nearly jumped out of my seat. "What's that?"

"The timer, obviously. It's letting me know our session is over. It was broken during your first session, but I managed to get it fixed."

"Oh." I looked around the room in a daze. It seemed like I'd only been here for a few minutes.

"You can't leave until you finish your drink. I'll not have alcohol wasted on my watch."

I dutifully swallowed the last of the Arrogant Bitch.

"See you next week?" she asked.

I hesitated. "Sure." To be honest, I was afraid to say no. Maybe this was how she kept her clientele. Therapy by fear.

"Namaste," she said with a friendly wave.

After therapy, I went to pay a visit to Janis Goodfellow. I'd visited her not too long ago, when I spoke with her about the youth spell on the town council. She'd been upset that they denied her request to grow nightshade and hemlock in her garden. She was an herbalist and considered it an important part of her vocation. Even if she wasn't the person who provided the nightshade to Will, she might know of other sources where he might have obtained it. Whether she would talk to me was another matter.

I didn't bother to knock on the front door. I walked around the house to the back garden where I knew I'd find her. Sure enough, she was tending to a group of plants along one of the many paths. In truth, it was a lovely garden. I just tried to make sure I didn't brush up against anything that might irritate my skin. Or kill me. Either one.

"If it isn't the most famous witch in Spellbound," Janis greeted me. She tilted back her sun hat to get a better view of me. "What brings you back here? Have I been accused of casting another spell?"

"Not quite," I said. I decided to get right to the point. "I'm defending a young werelion named Will." I paused to see if the name evoked a response, but her expression remained neutral. "He was found in possession of nightshade."

"Is that so? Well, that's interesting."

"Astrid would like to know if he obtained the nightshade from you," I said.

Janis barked a short laugh. "You mean Sheriff Astrid? Yes, I bet she would."

"You have to admit, if someone is selling nightshade and other poisonous plants on the black market, Spellbound might have a problem."

Janis returned her attention to the plants in front of her. "I'll admit no such thing. That's what happens when rules get in the way. People feel forced to do foolish things."

I folded my arms across my chest. "So are you saying that you helped this werelion?"

Janis smirked. "I've said nothing of the kind."

"Janis, I'm trying to help this person. It's my job to defend him. I'm not out to get you, despite what you think." I tried very hard to keep the irritation out of my voice, but I didn't think I was doing a very credible job.

She glanced skyward. "No familiar today? Was your owl unimpressed with the feeding grounds behind my house last time?"

"Never mind Sedgwick," I said. "I'm trying to do my job."

She met my gaze and I saw the flash of anger in her eyes. "And so am I. My job is herbalist. That means providing plants of all varieties, including deadly ones. They are an important part of herbology in a coven. The sooner Spellbound recognizes this, the better."

Janis had a whiff of a domestic terrorist about her. Was it possible she was spreading the possession of nightshade to make a point? If that was the case, then poor Will was going to pay the price for her zeal.

"Listen, if you change your mind, you know where to find me," I said. "I really do have his best intentions at heart. I don't want him to go to prison for five years for this."

"Just out of curiosity," she said, "where does *he* say he obtained the nightshade?"

"He claims that he found it grazing as a werelion in the countryside," I said. "But I can tell he's lying."

She nodded briefly. "Did he say what he intended to do with it?"

"Not yet," I said. "I hope to get that out of him during our next meeting. The more I know about the situation, the easier it is for me to defend him. I'd prefer that he only serves community service. He seems like a nice guy and I can tell he's hiding something."

"If I hear anything, I'll let you know," Janis said, and resumed tending to her plants.

I couldn't tell whether she was being polite to get rid of me or she actually meant it. Either way, that was my cue to leave.

"Thanks, Janis. I really do appreciate it."

Will Heath entered my office, looking as surly and shaggy as the last time I'd seen him. He walked straight to the chair and dropped into it like he had the weight of the world on his shoulders.

"Nice to see you again, Will," I said. "Have you had a chance to think about our last meeting?"

He shrugged. "Was I supposed to think about something in particular?"

"You were going to consider telling me where you acquired the nightshade," I said. "I went to see Janis Goodfellow. She wouldn't give me any concrete information, but my gut tells me that she wasn't the one who gave it to you."

"Probably not since I don't know her," he said. He kicked the leg of the chair with his heel in a nervous gesture.

"You really don't want to tell me where you got the nightshade, do you?" It was one thing not to want to rat out your dealer. Usually that was because you were more scared of the dealer than you were of going to prison. Will didn't seem scared to me, though. It was something I couldn't pinpoint.

"Will, I really want to help you. The only way I can do that is if I know the whole story. I would like it if you trusted me."

Will fidgeted in his seat. "I can't tell you."

"Why not? Are you protecting someone?" I mentally reviewed his file. He had two younger siblings. Maybe he was protecting one of them. "Did one of your younger brothers give you the nightshade? They're both minors. If it was one of them, they wouldn't face any prison time."

Will chewed his lip. "It wasn't my brothers." He clamped his mouth shut, unwilling to say more.

"Can you at least tell me what you planned to do with it? If I can convince the judge and the prosecutor that your intentions were good, that will go a long way toward a light sentence."

"My intentions were good. That's all I can tell you without saying too much."

"So you didn't intend to kill anyone with it?"

His fingers gripped the arms of the chair so tightly that I thought the wood would split. So he did intend to kill someone? Now I was completely baffled.

"Were you seeking revenge? Was this a pride thing?" I knew that the shifters in town had special rules that didn't necessarily jive with human rules. A perceived slight in the pack or pride was more serious than it would be in Lemon Grove, Pennsylvania.

"I wasn't seeking revenge," he said. "Any problems like that, I would go to the pride leader."

"Who is the pride leader for werelions?" I asked. Lorenzo Mancini was the alpha of the werewolf pack and a member of the town council. As the main shifter group in Spellbound, they wielded the most influence over the other shifters.

"His name is Anthony Shoostack."

"What has Anthony had to say about the charges against you?"

Will stared at his shoes again. "He's disappointed. It makes him look bad when one of us is in trouble."

"That's the pride mentality, isn't it?" It wasn't necessarily a bad thing. Social pressure was often a useful tool for keeping people in line.

"Where's the best place to find Anthony?" I asked.

Will's eyes popped open. "Why?"

"Because I'd like to talk to him," I said. "Is that a problem?"

He shook his head, his shaggy hair blowing every which way. "Not a problem. I just…Why?"

I leaned forward. "Because I'm trying to help you, Will, but you are not helping me. Maybe Anthony can shed some light on the situation."

"He can't," Will said quickly. Too quickly, in fact. Now I was more determined than ever to visit Anthony Shoostack.

"Where can I find him, Will?" I repeated, my voice firm and unyielding.

"He lives in the Glades," Will mumbled. "The house with the big garden gnome display."

Okay, that was not the description I was expecting. "Thanks, Will." I opened my file. "Now we may as well review the facts we have in the file, sparse they may be."

I needed to make a visit to Anthony Shoostack a priority. I hoped whatever secret Will was hiding, I could uncover it before his trial.

CHAPTER 9

"Today we would like to welcome Sophie's mother, Ariel, for a taster session on advanced mixology." Lady Weatherby stood in front of the long, wooden table and gestured toward the array of colorful beakers and bottles. "Ariel is one of the most experienced mixologists in the coven. Should you have any particular interests or curiosities, she is the witch to direct them to."

Ariel looked at Lady Weatherby and smiled. "Thank you for the kind introduction. Because this is an introductory class, I'll try to keep the terminology and explanations as simple as possible. If you'd like me to elaborate on anything, just let me know. I know that my Sophie often has follow-up questions." She winked at her daughter.

Millie's hand shot up. "Will we be able to try any of the potions today?"

"The word taster does imply trying it out, doesn't it? I do think we will be able to experiment a bit—under my close supervision, of course."

Millie looked pleased.

"I've brought the necessary ingredients for a number of

advanced potions. I thought I would let you choose the ones that you're most interested in." She touched a bottle in front of her. "We have ingredients for the Gibberish potion. Is anyone familiar with that one?"

Sophie raised her hand and her mother laughed softly. "Anyone other than my daughter?"

Sophie's hand dropped back to the table.

Millie was only too happy to step in. "It makes the speaker talk nonsense?"

Ariel nodded. "Yes. Ingesting this potion will cause the person to spew complete and utter nonsense."

I raised my hand. "Under what circumstances would you use a Gibberish potion?" Other than trying to make fun of someone, I couldn't see the point of it.

"One of the reasons these potions are part of advanced mixology is because they're not ones that you would encounter on a daily basis. These are magical cocktails you'd only want to mix under special circumstances."

Laurel frowned. "So it isn't advanced because it's hard to make? It's advanced because we'd rarely want to make it?"

"A little of both, I think," Ariel said.

"Can you give us an example of why someone would use the Gibberish potion?" Begonia asked.

Ariel looked thoughtful and then held up a finger. "I've got one. Someone I know used it on one of her children." She glanced at her daughter. "Mrs. Rhodes. You remember her, don't you? Anyway, this particular child of hers was getting into trouble for lying…"

Sophie rolled her eyes. "Kevin?"

"Yes, Kevin. This child refused to own up to it, no matter how many times he was caught. My friend mixed Gibberish potion into his lime fizz is one day and Kevin ended up speaking gibberish until he agreed in writing to mend his ways."

Gibberish as a form of punishment. I couldn't decide whether that was better than being banned from electronics like in the human word. Her example reminded me a little bit of Pinocchio and his growing nose.

"Another option for today is the Relax potion. One teaspoon of this in a person's drink and she will instantly turn to jelly." She paused. "Not literally, though. That's a different spell all together."

I raised my hand. "So is it similar to an anti-anxiety potion?" I took my dose every day to help me sleep and get through the day without vomiting, especially when I had to fly on a broom. I wasn't a fan of heights.

"This is more potent than anti-anxiety potion," Ariel said. "Relax might be used when someone is hysterical to calm them."

"How would we experiment with that one today if no one is hysterical?" Millie asked.

Without hesitation, Ariel whipped out her wand and said, "Them's the breaks/bring on the snakes." A nest of bright green snakes appeared at Millie's feet. She screamed and scrambled onto her chair as the snakes wrapped themselves around the base.

"Snakes," Millie screamed at a pitch high enough for every werewolf in town to hear. "They're going to kill me." Her face turned beet red as she began to hyperventilate.

I watched in awe as Ariel quickly mixed together three of the bubbling liquids on the table, uttered a magic word, and shoved a spoonful into Millie's mouth. She sucked it down without protest and dropped back into her chair, her head lolling to the side.

"Never fear/snakes disappear," Ariel said. The snakes vanished while Millie remained slumped in her chair, seemingly comatose.

Ariel chuckled. "It turns out someone was hysterical.

Good thing we had a Relax potion on hand to help." She winked at Millie.

No need to experiment with that one now.

"Let's move on," Ariel continued. "Another option is the Idealization potion. Can anyone tell me what that might be?"

Laurel raised her hand. "I read about this one in a story. It's when the drinker sees the best version of everyone around them."

"Very good, Laurel. Do you remember which story you read?"

Laurel drummed her fingers on the table. "It was a collection of short stories by Arabella St. Simon."

"Yes, our academy's namesake was a prolific writer as well as an exceptional witch."

"I think the story was called The Gift," Laurel said. "Does that sound right?"

Ariel nodded. "I know the story well. There once was an old hag who lived separate and apart from the rest of her coven. She didn't have a nice word to say about anyone or anything and preferred solitude. Sometimes other members of the coven would visit her and bring news from the community, but the old hag was never interested. She only wanted to see the bitter, not the better. Do you know the rest, Laurel?"

Laurel nodded. "One of the witches decided to brew her an Idealization potion. She mixed it into a cup of tea and the old hag began to see her visitors in a new light. Instead of viewing them as nosy neighbors, she saw them as caring witches who only wanted the best for her. It helped her realize that the world wasn't as negative as she perceived it to be."

The Idealization potion reminded me of rose-colored glasses. I raised my hand. "But if it's only an illusion, how is that a good thing?"

"No one said it was an illusion, Emma," Ariel said. "Think of it as a half-empty glass versus a half-full glass scenario. The old hag was choosing to view the world in a negative light, but the potion helped her to see the positive. When it finally wore off, she was able to mentally adjust her way of thinking. She welcomed visitors from then on and was able to see the best version of others and, as a result, became the best version of herself."

I studied the colorful beakers in front of me. "Maybe they should think about putting the Idealization potion in the pudding at the Spellbound Care Home," I suggested, only partially joking. I volunteered there fairly regularly with Daniel, so I was privy to a lot of the bitter attitudes of the residents. Not everyone, of course. There were plenty of charming and upbeat senior citizens, like Silas and Estella. Even former head of the coven Agnes was lively in her own crazy way.

"The next potion to consider is the Anti-Obsession potion," Ariel said. "Can anyone hazard a guess?"

Begonia raised her hand. "I guess it's to stop someone from obsessing about another person. Sort of like the opposite of a love spell."

"In part, yes. It doesn't necessarily need to be in relation to people, though. It can also be used to cure an obsession with a thing or a belief."

If only I could get my hands on something like that for Daniel, I thought to myself.

If there is an Anti-Obsession potion, Sedgwick's voice broke into my thoughts, *can't there be an Obsession potion?*

Normally I would be annoyed with Sedgwick for interrupting my thoughts during class, but, in this case, he raised a good point.

"Ariel," I interrupted. "Is there an opposite potion for all of the ones you've mentioned. For example, if you have an

Anti-Obsession potion, does that mean that there's an Obsession potion? Can you make someone obsessed with someone or something?"

"That is often the case," she said. "But an Anti-Obsession potion is generally more useful than an Obsession potion. If you think about it, an Obsession potion would only be for selfish purposes whereas an Anti-Obsession potion is more likely to be used to help someone overcome a mental obstacle."

An idea began to take shape. Was it possible that Daniel was under some kind of Obsession potion? Could that be why he was suddenly so smitten with Elsa again? Or was it just wishful thinking on my part?

"The final spell I brought ingredients for today is the Confusion potion," Ariel said. "A drop of this concoction will render the drinker completely and utterly confused. Sometimes, if you give too high of a dose, they won't even remember their own name. So you have to be careful with the dosage. The good news is that it does wear off."

My thoughts drifted back to the Obsession potion. "Do all of these potions you've mentioned wear off on their own? Do you have to keep giving them the potion in order for it to stay effective? Like if the person wasn't cured of their obsession with the first dose, would you give them more doses until you got the desired effect? Or if it wore off and they went right back to their obsession, would you keep giving it to them?"

Ariel regarded me carefully. "Those are very good questions, Emma. I guess I shouldn't be surprised that your mind is digging a little deeper. Yes, you would need to continue to give the potion to get the desired results. They all wear off after a certain amount of time. The amount of time, of course, depends on the dosage given and the size of the individual."

Like modern medicine. So if Elsa had given Daniel some kind of Obsession potion, then she would need to keep giving it to him or it would wear off.

Thanks, Sedgwick. Sometimes that little birdbrain of yours comes in handy.

I think someone needs a dose of an Anti-Insult potion, he said.

What do you mean? I just gave you a compliment.

If you say so, he replied. *You're too good to me. I promise not to get used to it.*

"So witches, which potion are we going to experiment with today?" Ariel asked. "Majority rules."

"I vote for the Idealization potion," Millie said, straightening her shoulders. "I'd like to know what the best version of me looks like to other people."

I stifled a laugh. Naturally she wanted to know how good the potion made her look. Typical Millie.

"I would like to try to the Relax potion," Begonia said. "Only because my noisy brothers kept me up last night. I'm really tired."

"Would the Idealization potion work on someone who wasn't bitter?" Laurel asked.

"Good question, Laurel," Ariel said. "Typically, the potions can only impact what isn't already there. So if you already see someone in a positive light, then nothing will change. But, for example, if you love the sunshine but hate the rain, then the potion might help you to see the positive attributes of the rain. It will mellow your negativity. Does that make sense?"

Laurel nodded. "I think it would be fun to try the Gibberish potion. I'd like to hear everyone's version of nonsense."

"Sophie?" her mother said. "Any preference?"

Sophie shook her head. "I see all of these at work at home. I'm happy to do what everyone else wants to do."

Ariel turned her attention to me. "That leaves you, Emma. Time to break the tie."

I couldn't decide. They all sounded interesting in their own way. "I wouldn't mind trying the Gibberish potion. It might be fun."

It took twenty minutes for our speech to return to normal once the potion wore off.

"I'm afraid I've taken us past your usual time," Ariel said. "My apologies. You're free to go."

I lingered while the other girls gathered their belongings and left.

"Can I help you pack up the ingredients?" I asked.

"That's kind, Emma," she said. "It's really just a flick of my wand." She tapped her wand on the table and the bottles and beakers shrank to a size small enough to fit in her travel bag.

"This never gets old," I said, admiring the bare table.

"Is something else on your mind?"

I cleared my throat. "We've talked about love potions in class before. Ginger said they work, but they're fairly complicated."

"They are," Ariel agreed. "That's why we don't run into too many issues with them, especially among the younger set."

"Is an Obsession potion easier?"

"Well, it's advanced mixology, but yes," Ariel said. "It's the next best thing to a love potion. The Obsession potion doesn't create love, only the illusion of love. It's an obsession rather than a deep and true emotion. There's no respect, no true devotion. It's more of a blind driving force. Does that make sense?"

I nodded. It made a lot of sense.

"How would you stop an Obsession potion from working?"

"Like I said, the potions wear off," Ariel said. "So if the person stops taking it, then the Obsession will cease to exist."

The gears were clicking away in my mind. "So you couldn't combat it with an Anti-Obsession potion?"

"I suppose you could. That might break the spell faster." She scrutinized me. "What's this about, Emma? Remember, this is advanced mixology we're talking about. I don't want you five girls running off to your secret lair and experimenting without supervision."

She knew about the secret lair? I wondered how many other witches in the coven knew. I hoped it was only because she was Sophie's mother.

"No, of course not. I just like to understand how these things work. It must be my lawyer brain."

Ariel smiled. "Yes, I must admit, it is nice to have an inquisitive mind in the class." She glanced around the room. "Not that the rest of them aren't inquisitive. They're all lovely." She blew kisses at the imaginary remedial witches. "Is my answer helpful at all?"

"Yes, Ariel," I told her. "More than you know."

CHAPTER 10

AFTER CLASS I drove to the Glades, where the werelion pride lived. There weren't nearly as many werelions as werewolves, so the community was more tight-knit. I could tell by Will's reaction that he didn't want me to visit Anthony Shoostack, which only made me more determined to speak with him.

I recognized the house right away thanks to the generous collection of garden gnomes in the front yard. I wondered if Amanda, Althea's younger sister, had made them.

I parked Sigmund in the driveway and waited a moment before opening the door.

Are you sure you want to do this? Sedgwick asked, circling above.

I peered out the window. *Where are you? I can't even see you.*

I'm keeping a safe distance, he said. *Werelions aren't opposed to eating owls.*

How high do you think they can jump? They're werelions not basketball players.

Even so, I'll be twenty feet up if you need me.

I opened the car door and walked toward the house. Before I reached the front step, I was greeted by two women. I couldn't decide which head of hair I envied more. The brunette had long, flowing locks that stretched down to her butt. Her hair was as shiny as a new copper penny. The other woman was blessed with red waves that reminded me of *The Little Mermaid*. The petty part of me resented them both. I absentmindedly touched my unruly dark hair and tried to be grateful that I wasn't bald.

"What can we do for you, new witch?" the redhead asked. It wasn't exactly a pleasant greeting. More of a demand.

"I'd like to speak with the head of your pride, if he's available."

"Is this about Will Heath?" the brunette asked.

"If it's all the same to you, I would rather keep the topic of the conversation private."

"Is it true you stood on Curse Cliff?" the redhead asked. She backed away slightly, and I got the sense that she shared Fabio's intense fear of the cliffside.

"It's true," I admitted. "To be fair, though, I didn't realize where I was standing at the time. Nothing bad has happened since then. I don't seem to have absorbed any negative energy."

The redhead looked unconvinced. "Fabio said you were weird."

I didn't have a response to that. In my mind, we were all a little bit weird. "So is Mr. Shoostack available?"

"Quit giving her a hard time and let her through," a voice boomed from inside.

I resisted the urge to smile triumphantly. The two self-appointed bodyguards moved so that I could pass.

"You both have beautiful hair," I called over my shoulder.

I couldn't say much for their personalities, but when I saw an opportunity to give a compliment, I preferred not to hold back.

The door to the house was wide open. "Mr. Shoostack?"

The head of the werelion pride sat in a recliner, drinking a bottle of beer and reading a book. He was long and lean with a luxurious head of bright white hair that made his sun-kissed skin appear even darker.

"You're reading *Pride and Prejudice*?" I asked incredulously. He hardly seemed the type to enjoy Jane Austen.

He shrugged. "I was misled by the word pride in the title. I thought it was about us. Once I started reading, though, I couldn't stop."

I laughed. "It's a very good book. I think you'll enjoy it."

He gestured to the sofa. "Have a seat, Emma. May I call you Emma?"

I nodded. "I'd like to speak with you about Will. I'll be defending him at his trial."

He set the book aside and gave me his full attention. "That Will is a good boy. His father died a couple of years ago and his mother basically checked out. He's been in charge of his siblings and doing a damn good job of it."

"Do you have any idea why he would want nightshade?"

"I wish I did," he said softly. "Don't like seeing any of ours in trouble. We try to take care of our own. His grandpa has been sick for a long time. We try to take turns caring for him so all of the work doesn't fall on Will's shoulders. It was bad enough to lose Will's father. That was sudden. But old Atlas has been hanging on for years now." He took a swig of beer. "No sign of departing us anytime soon either. The strongest weakling I've ever known, if you know what I mean."

"So Will is taking care of his two younger brothers, his mother, and his chronically ill grandfather?" Talk about a full plate for a twenty-year-old. My heart went out to him. "Does his grandfather live with him?"

"Yeah, they live three doors down in the rancher with the yellow door. I've tried to get Martha, that's his mother, to rejoin community life, but she's determined to live the rest of her days in a haze of misery."

"Has she considered therapy at all? I can recommend someone." I wasn't sure how Catherine Hall would handle a grieving werelion, but she'd certainly be tough enough to handle any hard-nosed shifter.

"The pride doesn't normally go in for that sort of thing," he admitted. "At this point, though, I'd be willing to entertain it for her. It's gone on too long. And now Will is suffering because of it."

"I get the sense that Will is protecting someone," I said. "He insists that his younger brothers had nothing to do with it. Is there any chance he's lying?"

Anthony shrugged. "There's always a chance. I don't know, though. He wouldn't say much to me either. You're right, though, in that he does seem to be keeping something to himself. He's a loyal werelion. I'll say that for him. A real source of pride for the pride." He chuckled at his own joke.

"Do you think it would be okay if I went to speak to his grandfather?"

"I'll do you one better, Emma. I'll walk you over there."

"Really?" I wasn't expecting full cooperation. Usually I got some pushback.

He grinned at me and stood. "We'll pretend we're taking a turn about the room like Mr. Darcy and Miss Bennett." He crossed the room to the couch and offered me his arm. "Shall we?"

I couldn't resist a smile. "That's very kind of you, Mr. Shoostack."

"Call me Anthony. We're not formal in the Glades."

We left the house and the scowling women behind us and walked along the lane until we reached the rancher with the yellow door.

"So what's wrong with his grandfather?"

"Some kind of lung disease," he said. "He's had it for so long that I don't even remember what he was like without it. Boyd has offered to come out on numerous occasions, but the old man refuses. Seems like he just wants to suffer endlessly."

"Some people just don't like to accept help," I said. "They don't want to seem weak."

Anthony nodded. "You definitely see that a lot in a were-lion pride. We're a bunch of stubborn sonsabitches. I don't think the old man realizes how hard he's made it on his family. Even if he'd just ease his suffering, it would help. That hacking cough must keep the whole family awake at night. Sometimes if my windows are open, I can hear it from my own bedroom."

The more I learned about Will, the sorrier I felt for him. I wanted to help him now more than ever.

Anthony rapped on the front door. "Atlas, you in there?"

"What about Will's mother?" I asked. "Isn't she home?"

"I saw her go past my house about an hour ago in lion form," he said. "She tends to leave the same time every day to go for a run in the countryside." He gave me a pointed look. "No one wants to break any ordinances."

"I would think that's good for her mental health," I said.

Before he could answer, the front door opened. A young boy stood in the doorway in his pajamas. He didn't look older than ten.

"Hi," I said. "Are you Will's younger brother?"

"I'm Nathan," he said. He glanced at Anthony. "Good afternoon, sir. Would you like to come in?"

"Those are some excellent manners, Nathan," I said. "We'd like to speak to your grandfather. Is he awake?"

A hacking cough from the other room made it clear that he was, indeed, awake.

"Grandpa," he yelled. "Anthony is here to see you with some lady."

Anthony patted Nathan on the head. "Why don't you fetch your grandpa a tumbler of whiskey and meet us in his room?"

Nathan nodded and ran off toward the kitchen. Anthony guided me to the room at the furthest end of the hallway. An old man with white flowing hair sat upright in bed. His face was worn and haggard, with dark circles under his eyes. He looked like he hadn't slept in a week.

"Anthony," Atlas managed to croak.

"How are you holding up, Atlas? I've got a friend of Will's here to see you."

I gave him a wave. "Technically, I'm his lawyer. I'm defending him against the nightshade charge. I was hoping to ask you a couple of questions."

"Lawyer?" Atlas glanced from me back to Anthony. "Will got arrested?"

I glanced at Anthony in surprise. No one had told his grandfather about the arrest?

"I suspect Will didn't want to worry you," Anthony said quickly.

Atlas stared at me. "Is he going to prison?"

"I hope not," I said. "My job is to defend him to the best of my ability. The problem is that he's stonewalling me. I can't help him if I don't have all the information."

The sound of a slamming door caught our attention. Will appeared in the doorway in a matter of seconds. He fixed his gaze on me, his brown eyes blazing.

"What are you doing here?" he demanded hotly. "I told you not to come."

"And I told you that I'm trying to help you," I said firmly. "That means talking to other people who know you."

Will strained not to shift into a lion. I could see the tension in his youthful features. "You need to leave. Now."

Anthony stepped between us. "Will Heath, you will end this now. As your pride leader, I insist that you answer your lawyer's questions honestly."

Will took a moment to decide his next move before storming out of the house. I chased after him, calling his name. By the time I reached the front yard, he'd shifted into lion form and taken off. Anthony joined me on the grass, clucking his tongue.

"I wish I could tell you more. I just think he's having a hard time."

It was understandable. He was only twenty years old with the responsibility of a forty-year-old. He hadn't learned to live his own life yet, but somehow he was responsible for four other lives.

"I'll give him some time," I said. "The trial isn't until next week."

Anthony shot me a sympathetic look. "In the meantime, I'll see what I can do."

While I was in the Glades, Astrid sent her owl to track me down. It seemed that Britta was busy at the station and Astrid needed a stand-in deputy with her to interview Donna Montrose, another suspect in the Ed Doyle murder case.

Donna was on the roof when we arrived, hovering above the chimney. Her wings fluttered at warped speed as she buzzed around the structure, taking copious notes.

"I guess a pixie makes sense for a job like this," I said. "It must be much easier for her to move around buildings than a satyr."

Astrid shrugged. "It didn't seem to deter Ed. From what I hear, he was very good at his job. Quick and thorough and always fair."

Astrid whistled to get Donna's attention. The pixie noticed us on the ground and made a beeline—or a pixieline—for us.

"Good day, Sheriff Astrid." She glanced at me and frowned. "And hello Girl I Don't Know." She gave Astrid a suspicious look. "Where's Britta? You haven't fired her already, have you?"

"No, she's holding down the fort at the station," Astrid said. "We had a few drunk and disorderlies come in. A were-ferret party got out of hand. Ricardo was dancing in the street wearing nothing but a strategically placed coconut shell."

Donna and I laughed. It was easy to imagine Ricardo drunk and disorderly—in the best possible way. He was far from a belligerent drunk.

"I'm Emma Hart," I said.

Donna's mouth formed a tiny 'o.' "The new witch from the human world."

"That's me." I gave her an awkward wave. I had a feeling I was going to be referred to as the new witch for the next century, if I managed to live that long. Instead of the FNG, I was the FNW.

"Do you need to get inside the building?" Donna asked. "It's only closed until I complete the final inspection." She referred to her notes. "If my calculations are correct, I should only be another twenty minutes."

"We don't need to get inside," Astrid said. "We need to talk to you."

"Me?" She seemed genuinely surprised. "What about?"

"Ed Doyle," Astrid said. "You were his apprentice. Isn't that right?"

Donna's expression softened. "Yes. Poor Ed. Such a tragedy."

"Not so much for you," I said. "Now you finally get to step into his shoes." Or hooves.

"Well, I have been waiting an awfully long time for my chance to shine," Donna admitted. "Ed was such an exemplary inspector. He never left any jobs for me to do."

"That must've been tough," Astrid said. "Here you are, working your wings off, trying to show the town that you can inspect a building like nobody's business. But there's diligent Ed, taking all the work."

Donna nodded. "It hasn't been easy. I've been training for what seems like forever. I'm so ready to do solo inspections."

Astrid smiled. "Well, now you can do as many solo inspections as you like."

Donna brightened. "I know. I guess if there has to be an upside to Ed's death, that's it." She frowned and quickly covered her mouth. "Oh no. That sounds dreadful, doesn't it? There shouldn't be an upside to Ed's death."

"You rode around town with him a lot to complete inspections, didn't you?" Astrid asked.

"All the time."

"And you helped move equipment like ladders and tools?" she continued.

"Yes, almost every day," Donna replied. "It was easy for me to move heavy and awkward things like ladders on account of my pixie dust."

"Do you know how Ed was killed?" I asked.

"He fell off a ladder," Donna said. "Between you and me, I heard someone pushed him, but no one says who it was."

"He wasn't pushed," Astrid said. "Someone tampered with his ladder."

Donna's brow lifted. "Who could possibly have done that? The ladder was either on the jalopy or with one of us…" She stopped talking, the realization settling in. "Oh. You think I tampered with the ladder?"

"We're only asking a few questions," Astrid said. "We don't think anything right now."

Donna didn't seem fond of the addition of the phrase 'right now.'

"Why would I kill Ed?" she demanded, her hands gripping her hips. "He and I worked well together. He taught me everything I know."

"He taught you everything, but then wouldn't let you use that knowledge independently. He hampered you," Astrid said. "And it made you very angry."

"Maybe you didn't mean to kill him," I said. "Just injuring him would get him out of the way long enough for you to shine. So you messed with the ladder thinking he might fall and break a leg." All About Ed instead of *All About Eve*.

"This is insane," Donna yelled. "I'd never hurt Ed. He was the gold standard of inspectors. Spellbound is a lesser place without him."

"Your fingerprints were all over the ladder," Astrid said, ignoring her outburst.

"Of course they were," Donna said, her wings agitated. "I told you I handled that ladder all the time."

"But you didn't notice any issues with it?" I asked.

"Of course not. I would have reported it."

"So you inspect buildings really well, but not so much your own equipment," I said.

If looks could kill, I'd have been a steaming pile of goo on the ground. "I had nothing to do with Ed's death. Nothing. If you'll excuse me, I have Ed's job to do. It's the best way to honor his memory." Her wings fluttered and she shot back to the roof.

Astrid and I exchanged looks.

"All residents should take their jobs so seriously," Astrid said.

I was inclined to agree.

CHAPTER 11

I STUMBLED INTO THE KITCHEN, rubbing the sleep from my eyes. I had been lost in a fog of sleep deprivation. I thought maybe it was time to increase the dose of my anti-anxiety potion.

"Good morning, my pet," a scratchy voice said.

I jumped back, knocking into the counter and dispatching the cookie jar onto the floor. It broke into several large pieces.

"Not Mr. Cookie," Gareth cried. He bent down to pick up the pieces.

"I'm so sorry," I said. "I wasn't expecting company at this hour." I paused and looked curiously at Lyra Grey, the middle Grey sister. "How did you get here?" Usually I had to go and collect her. Her cave was on the outskirts of town and much too far to walk.

"I had an appointment in town this morning," Lyra said. "The doctor was kind enough to send a jalopy for me."

"And they let you take it anywhere you like?" It was weird enough to think of an ophthalmology shuttle. Now they were giving her free reign?

"The jalopy isn't here, dearest," she said. "I asked the driver to drop me here after the appointment. I told him that you would drive me home later." She scratched her chin with her long, straggly fingernail. "He seemed quite pleased, he did. I got the distinct impression that he did not want to drive back to the cave."

Who could blame him? That cave was one of the scariest places I'd visited in Spellbound and that was saying something.

"Are you and Gareth having an impromptu lesson?" It was only then that I noticed Gareth had managed to pick up all the broken pieces of the cookie jar and place them on the kitchen counter. "Stars and stones. You moved multiple objects at once." I couldn't keep the amazement from my voice. Gareth had made impressive strides since he began working with Lyra.

Gareth smiled proudly. "Aye, we've been working on this sort of skill."

"He'll be cooking in no time, he will." Lyra glanced around the kitchen. "Speaking of cooking, I would not mind a bite to eat, not at all."

"Well, I'm all out of raw headless chickens, but I might have a cooked drumstick if that interests you." It wasn't my ideal breakfast, but then again I hadn't been living in a cave for the last century.

Lyra's tongue darted out and flicked her upper lip before disappearing back into her mouth. "Yes. A drumstick would do nicely, it would. Any Goddess Bounty to wash it down with?"

"I'm afraid not," I said. "But I'd be happy to make you a cup of tea."

"Tea," she repeated. "That reminds me. I've been wondering whether I should drop in on my old friend

Octavia Minor. I haven't seen that harpy in a unicorn's age. Is she as ugly as I remember?"

To be fair, I wasn't sure which one of them had been beaten harder with the ugly stick. Lyra Grey definitely had better hair, but Octavia Minor had the glowing skin that came with not living in a cave for a century. She also had all of her teeth and two eyes, which Lyra had only recently acquired thanks to me.

"The Minor house is just up the road," I said. "I doubt they would mind a visit from an old friend."

"Join me, you will," she said.

I glanced down at my heart pajama bottoms and fluffy bunny slippers. "You know, I would love to, but I've only woken up and I think they prefer their visitors to be appropriately dressed."

Gareth folded his arms and smirked. "Don't be silly, Emma. Lyra will wait. Run up now and get changed."

After all I'd done for him, Gareth wanted to throw me under the trampling legs of the harpies. I'd remember this the next time he begged me to organize the contents of my closet by color.

"Perhaps later," Lyra said. "It wouldn't be fair to you, vampire. After all, I came for another lesson, not a social call."

"And he's made such incredible strides since you came along," I said. "I certainly wouldn't want him to miss out today." When Lyra turned her back, I stuck out my tongue at Gareth. He narrowed his eyes in response.

"Let me grab a quick breakfast and I'll get out of your way," I said.

"Don't forget to make our guest a cup of tea," Gareth said.

"I think not, vampire," Lyra said. "I think today that will be part of your lesson. Wait until she leaves, we will."

I stifled a satisfied smile as I hurried about the kitchen,

preparing a bowl of burstberry oats and tea. I rushed from the room as quickly as I could. From the dining room table, I heard snippets of the lesson.

"Not like that. Like this," I heard Lyra say tersely. To his credit, not once did I hear Gareth complain.

I quickly finished breakfast and rushed upstairs to shower and dress. By the time I came downstairs, they'd moved into the living room where Lyra was demonstrating how to start the fire.

"Why does he need to know that?" I asked. "It's not like he ever gets cold."

She fixed her gaze on me and smiled. Her perfect white teeth were at odds with her aging face. "But one day you may want him to start the fire for you. Or for that lovely feline companion of his." She surveyed the room. "Where is the small beast? Usually he does not stray far from my feet."

Lyra was right. Magpie had taken a shine to her and, during her visits, could often be found within close proximity to her. It was baffling to me, but I didn't question it. There was a lid for every demented pot.

As if on cue, Magpie poked his head up from one of the dining room chairs and rested his chin on the table.

"There is that most majestic creature," she said, crossing the room to scratch behind his half-chewed ear. "You are the handsomest of fellows, you are."

"Any thoughts about when you'd like to go home?" I asked.

Lyra peered at me, still scratching Magpie's head. I was almost certain I heard the faint sound of purring. "I thought we might stop and see the Minors on our return journey."

I hesitated. I'd promised to meet Markos to discuss his conversation with Astrid and it was a long drive to the cave and back. And it wasn't like I could decide when it was time to leave the home of the harpies. That would be a decision made for me if I valued my life.

"I think Emma has important plans this afternoon," Gareth said, and I sighed inwardly with relief. He must've felt guilty about his earlier comment.

"Stay long, we won't," Lyra said. "Until next time, vampire. Come along, human."

We'd have to work on her manners. Identifying others by their species out loud probably wasn't the most tactful way of addressing someone. I tried to imagine myself walking around town saying things like, "Hey, harpy. Where's my tea?" Or "Good morning, fairy. Work any magic today?" Or my personal favorite, "Hey, vampire. Bloodsucking hard or hardly bloodsucking?"

"Maybe you and I could talk about the case later," I told Gareth. "I wouldn't mind an extra set of ears." Gareth's personal experiences with the residents were often as helpful as his experience as the public defender.

"Absolutely," he said. "You know me. Dying to be useful."

"Or just dead," I said, giving him a cheeky grin. "I'll meet you at the car, Lyra." As she left the house, I ran upstairs to grab my handbag. When I came back down, Gareth was hovering by the front door. "What are you doing?"

"Thinking," Gareth said.

I groaned. "That makes me nervous."

He chuckled. "I usually say the same about you."

I eyed him curiously. "What are you thinking about?"

He sucked in a breath and I knew I wouldn't like what he had to say. "You should invite the Grey sisters to poker night."

I choked. "I'm sorry. My ears must be clogged. I thought you just told me to invite the frightening Grey sisters to poker night."

"I did."

I tried to push against his chest, but my hands went straight through him. "Who are you and what have you done with my grumpy vampire ghost roommate?"

"I've been getting to know Lyra," he said. "I think she and her sisters are ready to socialize more. They seem lonely, even though they have each other."

"No one exiled them to the cave," I said. "They've chosen to live that way."

"You're the one who's always trying to be inclusive," he said accusingly. "Why is it so shocking when I make a suggestion?"

He had a point. "But do we have to invite all three? Can't we just start with Lyra and work our way up to three over time?"

"It's up to you," he said. "It's your poker night. Perhaps you could invite Althea and her sisters. It would be like a family reunion."

"Are you trying to kill me? Althea told me that, even though their cousins, they don't exactly get along." Not to mention the house would be full of my friends who would probably be scared witless to be sharing the table with six of the most dangerous women in Spellbound.

"As I said, it's up to you. I think it would be a nice gesture, though."

The idea also made me uncomfortable because the Grey sisters were the only ones aside from Daniel who knew my secret. What if one of them drank too much Goddess Bounty and spilled the beans to everyone at poker night? That would be disastrous. Then again, the expression on Gareth's face was so sincere and he rarely asked me for any favors. He was dead and here I was living in his house and taking over his job—it hardly seemed fair to refuse him.

"I'll decide after tea with the Minors," I said.

"Assuming you live through it," Gareth said with a wry smile.

I shot a disapproving look over my shoulder as I went to join Lyra in the car.

The look on Phoebe Minor's face when she opened the door was priceless. "Wings and wands. I haven't seen you in…" She tapped her talon-like fingernails on the doorframe. "Barnaby's funeral was it?"

"May we come in or have social graces changed dramatically since the last time I was here?" Lyra asked.

If one of them began to pee all over the floor in a show of dominance, I was out of there in a flash.

"Please come in," Phoebe said with mock sincerity. "Emma knows I'm always happy to see her."

I wasn't convinced that was true. It was probably meant as a dig at Lyra.

We entered the tchotchke-filled foyer while Phoebe yelled to the rest of her family. "Loving family. We have unexpected visitors. You'll never guess who."

"Never guess?" A bitter voice said from the next room. "I can smell her toxic fumes from here. There's only one family I know that smells like a mix of sewage, booze, and supper. The question is—which Grey sister is it?"

We followed Phoebe into the sunroom to see Octavia Minor, the matriarch harpy. At first glance, I thought she was knitting until I realized she was not adding fluff to an object, but removing it. I swallowed hard. Apparently she was skinning a rabbit in the comfort of her own home.

"I should've known I'd find you engaged in a worthwhile activity," Lyra said.

Octavia held up the rabbit by the feet. "You don't catch many of these around that cave of yours, do you?"

"You would be surprised to know what we find, you would," Lyra said.

Marisol Minor swept into the room, wearing a halter top sundress more appropriate for a twenty-year-old living in the 1950's. Her blond hair was fixed in a bun and she wore enough makeup to withstand a nuclear blast. "Can I offer anyone tea and finger sandwiches?"

Before Lyra could ask the question I knew was burning on her lips, I leaned over and whispered, "Not actual fingers." I quickly realized that Lyra was probably disappointed by the clarification.

"Tea and treats for everyone," Octavia said. She dropped the rabbit into a nearby basket and turned her attention to us. "What good deeds have we done to earn a visit from you? Next you'll tell me the curse has been broken and the borders are open."

"Not so fortunate as that, I'm afraid," Lyra said. She took the seat beside Octavia, which was just as well because I preferred to sit as far away from her as possible.

"Darcy, Calliope, Freya," Octavia bellowed. "Come and say hello to our guests."

One by one they appeared, each one more human and 'normal' than the last.

"Miss Grey," Calliope said. "It's so good to see you again."

Phoebe studied Lyra's face. "Have you had work done? Something's different."

"It's her eyes, nitwit," Octavia said. "She actually has two of her own now."

"And these," Lyra added, showing off her teeth.

Phoebe staggered backward. "What in Nature's name...?"

Lyra nodded toward me. "The human paid me a debt."

Octavia cast a suspicious look in my direction. "What kind of debt?"

Since Gareth's ghost was no longer a secret, I felt

comfortable telling them. "She's helping Gareth learn new skills as a ghost. I offered her a makeover of sorts in exchange for her trouble."

Phoebe nodded somberly. "A fair deal."

"How have your sisters dealt with the change?" Marisol asked, carrying a tray of treats into the room and setting it on the table. She quickly returned with the tray of tea.

"Yes," Freya said, "if I suddenly woke up and my family had shed their talons and wings permanently, I don't know how I would feel."

"She isn't giving something up," Phoebe said. "She's gaining something positive."

"So what news have you to share?" Lyra asked, as she accepted her cup of tea. She took a grateful sip and I noticed the expression of serenity that passed over her wrinkled features. "I suspect the human doesn't know nearly as much town gossip as the harpies."

"Too true," Octavia said with a deep and throaty laugh. "She's too busy trying to save everyone in town, one resident at a time. Eventually she'll learn it's a thankless task and stop her efforts."

That seemed harsh commentary on the residents of Spellbound. Then again, I wasn't as old or bitter as Octavia Minor. Maybe if I lived to her ripe old age, my attitude would be different.

"The town building inspector was murdered recently," Darcy said.

"Such a tragedy," Calliope said. "Everyone liked Ed."

Octavia snorted. "Not everyone, apparently, or he wouldn't be dead."

"Has Sheriff Astrid narrowed down the suspects?" Darcy asked me.

"Sheriff Astrid?" Lyra queried. "Who is Sheriff Astrid?"

"She's a Valkyrie," Calliope said. "She was the deputy for many years."

"And she's very capable," I added.

"A woman in charge of law enforcement," Lyra mused. "Spellbound is changing, it is."

"Women have always been powerful in the paranormal world," Phoebe countered. "A female sheriff is nothing new."

"Still," Lyra said. "Nice to see, it is." She gave me a pointed look. "Women of true strength and power are few and far between."

I coughed and Darcy thrust a cup of tea into my hands.

"I wonder whether the sheriff has been to see Serena Bogan," Darcy said.

The name didn't ring any bells. "Why?" I asked.

"I was in Glow having my nails done and Serena was at the station next to mine telling her manicurist all about the argument. When she left, the manicurist told us that Serena had tried to bribe him, but he refused to take the money and threatened to report her."

Wow. I'd have to tell Astrid so she could check the records for a report of the incident.

"Thanks, Darcy. That's helpful," I said.

"Like you, I feel it's important to do my part for the community," Darcy said primly.

Phoebe rolled her eyes.

"Maybe if you'd spend more time doing your part for a single man instead of the whole community, you'd actually be married to one," Octavia said.

Darcy bristled. "Please don't start, grandmother."

"Take a page out of this one's book," Octavia continued, gesturing to me. "She's got the damsel in distress routine down pat. The males are sniffing around her in droves. She'll need to beat them off with her wand."

Now it was my turn to bristle. "I beg your pardon. I don't

act like a damsel in distress and I certainly don't feel that being unmarried makes any woman a failure." The sharp words were out of my mouth before I could stop them.

The room fell silent. The three youngest Minors became preoccupied with the view from the sunroom windows. Octavia studied me, her eyes cruel and unrelenting.

"Tell us your secret," Octavia said, her voice low and serious.

Fear gripped me. My secret? She knew about my secret? "I don't know what you mean," I stammered.

"An army of potential suitors at your beck and call is almost better than sex," Octavia continued. "I want to know how you manage it. What's your secret?"

I relaxed slightly. "According to Gareth, it's because I'm new in town and no one is ever new. I'm a novelty."

"Well, nothing we can do about that," Phoebe said.

"But you're the only harpies in town," I said. "Maybe you can capitalize on that somehow."

"Men don't exactly come running when they hear the word 'harpy,'" Darcy said. "In fact, I'm fairly certain they run in the opposite direction."

"That's why we spend so much time in our human forms," Calliope added. "In the hope of attracting a mate."

"But you want to be yourself," I said. "People can sense when you aren't genuine, even if they can't put their finger on the problem."

"You think if we're more comfortable in our harpy form that we should stop looking human?" Freya asked, glancing around the room. "I'd be on board with that idea. I feel naked without my wings."

"I don't know," I replied. "I mean, I have one form and it's human, so I think you're the only one who can answer that question." *Just please wait until I've left to turn hideous. My tea and finger sandwich needs to digest.*

"The witch makes a good point, she does," Lyra said.

"Says the woman with two eyes and a full set of teeth," Phoebe griped.

Lyra dragged a long fingernail down the back of my arm and I shuddered. It was like being touched by death. "I believe it is time to bid them farewell. My sisters await my return."

I tried to disguise my relief. "Of course. Thank you for a lovely visit."

"Where are you going, Freya?" Marisol asked her youngest daughter.

"To the widow's walk to change form," Freya replied. She turned to me and smiled. "I'll screech to you from the sky."

Lucky me.

On the drive back to the cave, I remembered Gareth's request and decided to honor it. Lyra didn't seem so scary once I'd spent time with her, and it was sad to picture the Grey sisters living so long in isolation. After all, the harpies that weren't miserable seemed to be the ones more involved in the community.

"If you and your sisters aren't busy on Thursday evening, I'd like it if you came to poker night at my house."

Lyra's white and grey eyebrow lifted a fraction. "What is poker? Is it a ritual from the human world?"

I laughed softly. "Something like that. I won't be able to drive you because I'll be hosting, but I can send a jalopy for you."

Lyra didn't even hesitate. "We accept your offer," she said, opening the car door. She tapped the hood gently as she headed toward the mouth of the cave. "Until next time, Sigmund."

I wasn't sure she meant for me to hear that. Regardless, I found myself humming all the way back into town.

CHAPTER 12

I WAS SURPRISED to arrive at Faraway Field and find it empty. Markos was even later than I was. The sound of a magical engine caught my attention as Markos pulled over behind Sigmund and rushed from the car.

"I'm sorry I'm late," he said, panting. "I got caught up in a business matter." He still appeared distressed.

"Something to do with Ed's murder?"

He shook his head. "No, still trying to reconcile these damn figures. I don't want to bore you with that. Or at least let us get to know each other better before I bore you." He grinned.

"You had your meeting with Astrid, didn't you?" I asked.

"I did." He raked a hand through his thick brown hair. "It was stressful, I'll admit."

"If it's any consolation, I have a lead for her. Something Darcy Minor overheard in the salon."

"I'll accept any bit of gossip as a potential lead at this point," he said. "I didn't like the way Britta was looking at me."

I laughed. "Not many people do."

"Enough about stressful topics," he said. "Let's take a walk through the field on this gorgeous day and enjoy each other's company."

"Sounds like a great idea," I said. "Where's the footpath?" There were bursts of color as far as the eye could see.

"Over here." Markos beckoned me to a hidden path.

I breathed in the fragrant air. "These flowers smell divine."

"Feel free to pick any you like," he said. "They'll look beautiful on a mantel in your living room."

"Maybe when we're about to leave." We continued to walk in companionable silence.

"Tell me about the human world," he said. "Is it as delightful as I remember?"

"I guess it depends on your definition of delightful," I said. "I think it's like anywhere. Some places are wonderful. Others are pits to avoid." I paused. "So I guess you tended to be in your human form back when you were in the human world."

"Yes, I've had the ability to take two forms for quite a long time. It was a necessity at a certain point. A matter of survival. Humans became less and less tolerant of anyone too different. In some ways, I think Spellbound is a blessing."

"But there are other paranormal towns all over the world like this one. Why not live in one of those?" The only difference between those places and Spellbound was that those residents were free to come and go at will. Spellbound was the one with magical boundaries that kept everyone trapped inside.

"I've done both," Markos said. "For a long time, I lived in regular human towns in Greece. Eventually I moved to a paranormal town in Southern California. The climate was closer to what I was used to."

I laughed. "Then how did you end up in the Pocono

Mountains in Pennsylvania?" You couldn't get much further from the Mediterranean environment.

"I followed a young lady, of course," he admitted. "Why else do we do foolish things but for love?"

I knew that all too well. Even though I didn't know Daniel when I tried to rescue him from jumping off the cliff, he was the reason I was stuck here in the first place. It somehow seemed fitting that I fell in love with him.

"I see my neighbors and their harpy forms," I said. "Do you ever walk around in your minotaur form?"

Markos became fixated on the ground. "Not really. In the early days, I would walk around town when the mood struck me. Things have changed here over time, though. In some ways, it parallels my experience in the human world."

I frowned. "Why? It doesn't make sense. This is the one place all of you should feel free to be yourselves. Everyone here has something supernatural about them. Wings, horns, bumpy faces, fangs. Why should anyone feel ashamed?"

Markos looked thoughtful. "I really don't know. Sometimes I think it's because the majority of residents here still resemble humans. The witches, wizards, elves, fairies, vampires. The list goes on. Their nonhuman features are so subtle that it isn't the same as for a minotaur or a harpy."

"What about George?" I asked, thinking of the giant yeti. "He certainly looks different."

"That's true," Markos said. "And George is very well-liked in the community."

I smiled. "And so are you, in case you haven't noticed. I don't think I've heard a bad word about you since my arrival."

Markos seemed pleased. "Is that so? Well, I guess that explains your willingness to be friends with me."

I noticed that he went out of his way not to say 'to date me.'

"I tend to be a good judge of character," I said.

"Were you always like that? Did you know to stay away from the man in the car asking you to find his lost puppy?"

"I think it's a skill I developed over time," I said. "When you lose your parents at a young age, you tend to lose a bit of trust in the world. At least I did. It forced me to pay attention to people, to try to understand their motives. I questioned a lot of things."

"And I suppose that skill only became more developed once you were a lawyer," he said.

Flowers bent in the breeze and brushed against my legs. The field was so peaceful and calm. I'd have to remember this place.

"I hate to say it, but I really became jaded after only a couple of years. I definitely saw the negative side of people fairly quickly."

"What kind of law did you practice?" he asked. "I remember hearing that you had no criminal law background."

"No, I worked in public interest law. I often represented people who got tangled up in a bureaucratic mess. They didn't necessarily have the education or knowledge required to get themselves out of it."

"So you weren't raking in the cash like corporate lawyers or litigators, I imagine," he said.

I suppressed a smile. "No, I certainly can't say I was raking it in. In fact, I was struggling to pay my bills on top of my student loans. Even though I went to a state university for law, I still had to take loans to foot the whole bill, plus living expenses. You can't have a job when you're in law school. There simply isn't time to do both."

Markos studied me intently. "Were you always such a hard worker?"

"I had to be," I said. "There wasn't any other choice. My

grandparents were dead at this point and it wasn't like they had money to leave me. We weren't exactly wealthy. Anyway, it doesn't matter. You do what you have to do to survive. You know that."

He nodded gravely. "I like to think it builds character."

Me too. "So who was the lady you followed to Spellbound?" I asked. "Or am I overstepping?"

"It isn't possible to overstep with me," he said. "That's something I want you to know. I'm pretty thick-skinned and I know you would never say anything intentionally cruel or hurtful."

I softened. "So who was she?"

He inhaled deeply, gazing skyward. "Her name was Eden. I met her in California. She was very beautiful, which was obviously the first thing I noticed about her. People say looks don't matter, but they can certainly get someone's attention."

I was inclined to agree. Although my love for Daniel developed once I got to know him, it was definitely his looks that first drew me to him. Literally drew me right out of my car and almost into a lake.

"What was she? A fairy?"

"No, she was a succubus."

Oh, that explained it. "That must've been an interesting relationship." I wasn't even sure if the succubus was capable of maintaining a relationship with one person. It seemed like their needs were too overwhelming. Then again, I didn't really know one well enough. Only what I'd read in books.

"It was, needless to say, an intense relationship. When she announced she was going to see her sister in Valley Ridge, I jumped at the chance to join her."

"She didn't mind?" I queried.

"I think she believed I wouldn't want to come. I loved the California sunshine and I knew the weather would be different here."

I glanced up the warm, shining sun. "Turns out that it's not so different after all, huh?"

"Only since the curse took hold," he said. "When it was still Valley Ridge, we had all the seasons. Lots of snow."

As you would expect in the Poconos. "So what happened? Is she still here?"

"She got trapped here, same as me." He lowered his gaze. "Eventually she died."

"Oh, Markos. I'm so sorry. Do you mind me asking what happened?"

He gave me a rueful smile. "I told you. You can't overstep with me." He paused, remembering Eden. "We paranormals are pretty good at fighting off diseases. We have magic, healers, our own immunities. Incubi and succubi are more prone to pick up infections because of the nature of their...Well, their nature."

I think I knew what he was trying to say. "But if you were her partner, how...?"

He gave me a hard look and I understood. She'd been unfaithful. And she paid a steep price for it.

"She didn't just lose me," he said, shaking his head. "She lost her life."

I felt a rush of sympathy for him. "Markos, that's terrible. I'm so sorry. There was nothing anyone could do?"

"There would have been, had she confessed sooner," he said. "But she tried to keep the truth from me. She was so afraid of my reaction. It cost her her life."

"Have you been in love since Eden?" I asked.

"No," he said sadly. "I like to think I'm open to the possibility, but, after all this time as a bachelor...I must be more closed off than I realize."

"You don't seem closed off to me," I said. "You seem very honest and comfortable to be with."

He stopped walking. "That's because I'm in human form.

You probably wouldn't say that if I were in my minotaur form."

I gazed up at him. "Is it possible for you to turn into your minotaur form at will?"

"I can shift between them at will," he said. "Why?"

"I'd like to see if I'm comfortable with the real you," I said.

He splayed his hands. "This is the real me. Whenever you speak to me, you get the real me. The outside is just a shell."

"That may be true, but I'd still like to see you in your natural state. If we're going to get to know each other better and become good friends, I don't think we should hide who we are."

He hesitated. "Things are going well. I don't want to put you off."

"Have you seen what I live with? Magpie is allegedly a cat. Trust me, your minotaur form is nothing."

He chuckled. "That is one unfortunate beast." He sucked in a breath. "You're sure about this? What is seen cannot be unseen."

I nodded vigorously. "Bring on the horns."

He closed his eyes and I watched as bones began to crack and shift.

"It sounds painful," I said. "It doesn't hurt, does it?"

He gestured with his hand to wait a moment and I realized that he couldn't speak during the shift. Hair began to sprout all over his body and it reminded me of when I'd seen Alex shift from human to werewolf form. He'd gotten stuck in his half form because of a potion he drank. I shuddered remembering the pain he'd suffered.

Horns broke through his head. Not little nubs like the satyrs or centaurs had, but huge twisted horns larger than any I'd seen in Spellbound. His face changed from fully human face to something between a man and a bull. A ring appeared in his newly wide nose. His muscular arms and legs grew even bulkier. He was already extremely tall in human form. Now I had to crane my neck even further to see him. When the transformation was complete, he kneeled down, his cloven hooves hidden behind him.

"So what's the verdict?" he asked. "On the hideous scale of one to ten, where do I fall?"

I reached up to touch his horn. "May I?"

He lowered his head slightly and I ran my fingers along the curve of the horn. It was beautiful.

"I didn't know there was a hideous scale," I said. "Whatever it is, you're not on it."

"You don't have to be nice, Emma," he said. "I'm a realist. I can take it."

I moved from the horn to touch his face. The fur looked rougher than it actually felt. It was soft like a cashmere blanket. I imagined he could keep someone quite warm on a chilly night.

"Thank you for having the courage to show me," I said. "I feel like you must trust me and that means a lot."

"Of course I trust you," he said. "You've never given me any reason to doubt you."

"But we don't know each other that well," I said. "Aren't you hesitant to trust people after what Eden did?"

"Eden succumbed to her nature," he said. "I try not to color every woman with the same brush."

"And yet you're still a bachelor. A very popular, desirable bachelor." I studied him, not the least bit afraid. "You know what, Markos? As social as you are, I don't think you've been willing to give someone else a real chance."

His thick, furry finger touched my cheek. "Maybe not, but I am now."

"I understand you've been out with Markos again," Catherine said.

"Holy Therapist Spy," I said. "Do you have someone tailing me?"

"Of course not. I'm a therapist. People pass along information every day."

"Yes, I've been out with Markos. He's got a lot going on right now." Not to mention emotional baggage. "I think he could really use a friend."

"Are you sure that's wise? Doesn't he have a romantic interest in you?" Catherine fixed me with her unrelenting stare. Unlike Demetrius's sexy vampire gaze, Catherine's was intimidating and, at times, downright frightening.

"I've been very clear with him where the boundaries are," I said. "I'm not going to abandon him during a time in need just because he might want to kiss me."

"And how are you feeling about the engagement? Have you had more time to process?"

"I've been working on a theory, if you must know," I said. I'd been doing my best to keep it to myself, but Catherine was bound by client confidentiality. If I told her, she would be duty bound not to reveal it to anyone.

"A theory? What kind of theory?" She looked genuinely intrigued. Anything to spice up a boring therapy session.

"You have to promise not to tell anyone," I said. "I don't care how drunk you are."

She pretended to lock her lips. "It's in the therapist vault."

I leaned forward and lowered my voice. "I think Elsa may be using some kind of Obsession potion to keep Daniel's interest." I sat back and waited for the information to settle.

Catherine hesitated briefly before bursting into laughter. "Nice try. Is that type of wishful thinking how you get through life?" She picked an imaginary piece of lint from her shirt. "I suppose it is. Emma, you know what Elsa Knightsbridge looks like, right? It's hardly surprising that he's obsessed with her."

I balked. "But she's awful. Everyone thinks so. She's spoiled and mean. She left Jasper in the lurch the second she got her hooks into Daniel."

"Meow," Catherine said, pretending to scratch the air. "I didn't know you had a catty bone in you. Consider myself schooled."

"I am not being catty," I said, hearing the exasperation in my voice. I didn't care. I was exasperated. "I think she's mixing a potion in his drink every day. I'm going to try and figure out how she's keeping him under her spell."

"Have you shared your theory with anyone else?" Catherine asked.

I nodded. "Sedgwick agrees with me."

Catherine arched an eyebrow. "Your familiar? That's your support?"

"Not just Sedgwick," I said. I felt my cheeks getting redder by the second. "I swear to you that he is not himself. Daniel and I spoke about her the day we ran into her. I left the house when they were mid-conversation and, by the time he left, he was smitten. It doesn't make sense."

Catherine tapped her red fingernails on the arm of the chair. "Emma, let me diagnose this. You're being delusional. You need to let him go. Markos is a perfectly nice option. You should really consider him for that tight butt alone."

"The way you considered other suitors besides Lord Gilder?" I snapped. I hadn't intended to mention him. I was going to keep what I'd noticed to myself, but the information burst out of me in anger.

Catherine reeled back. "What are you talking about?"

"I saw you at the engagement party. I saw the way you were watching him." I recognized that look because I wore it so often myself. "You're in love with Lord Gilder. He's your unrequited love."

Catherine tipped back her glass and drained it. Then she slowly set the empty glass on the coffee table in front of her. "Lord Gilder is the head of the vampire coven. I have great admiration for him. That's all."

I folded my arms and glared at her. "You can admire someone and still want to get into his pants." I knew this all too well.

"Emma Hart, bite your tongue or I'll bite it for you. I haven't had fresh blood in ages."

"How long have you felt this way?"

"I told you," she insisted. "I feel nothing except admiration and respect."

"And sexy thoughts," I added. "I told you that I saw the way you looked at him. You were undressing him with your eyes. I'm pretty sure you even ran your tongue across your upper lip. You definitely wanted to bite him in a sexy way."

Catherine jumped to her feet and stomped over to the bar to pour herself another drink. "Stop it. You're being absurd."

"Am not. How did you meet him?"

"He was my neighbor when I first moved to Valley Ridge, before it became Spellbound. I had just gotten out of a bad relationship and was living on my own for the first time in ages. I'd forgotten how to take care of myself. It was embarrassing. It was then that I swore I would never rely on another person ever again." With her eyes and mouth briefly closed, she appeared entirely human.

"I take it he was a helpful neighbor," I said.

"More than helpful," she said, heaving a deep sigh. "He went out of his way for me. He knew I was too proud to ask for help, so he would come around and make up reasons to do things for me. He always made it seem like it was beneficial to him in some way." A faint smile touched her lips. "As the town grew, he ended up moving elsewhere. The head of the coven needed a more impressive place, you see."

"Spellbound is a pretty small town," I said. "It isn't like he moved hundreds of miles away. Why did that change anything?"

"It was the daily interaction that stopped," she said. "I realized how much I missed it. Running into him at coven meetings or at the Wish Market wasn't the same."

"He isn't with anyone," I said. "What kept you from asking him out?"

Catherine shook her head adamantly. "Lord Gilder is a highly respected member of the community. He's on the town council. He's the head of our coven. He's much too important for someone like me."

"Someone like you? What's that supposed to mean? Catherine, you are a tough, independent, highly educated woman. You don't take minotaur shit from anyone. I would think those are valued traits."

Catherine downed another drink. "I appreciate your support, Emma. But I know Lord Gilder well. If he'd been interested in me, he would have made it clear long ago."

"You don't think stopping by to help you every day was an indication? Maybe he thought you didn't return his feelings, so when he moved away, he didn't pursue you."

"I think we should focus on your crackpot theory," Catherine said. "That's far more entertaining."

The sound of screeching bats indicated that we'd reached the end of the session.

I glanced at Catherine. "This conversation isn't over."

She gestured toward the exit door. "It is now."

CHAPTER 13

ASTRID, Britta, and I walked over to a new building two blocks north of the Wish Market. The noise level told us that a construction crew was hard at work. It was quite a different sight from construction crews in the human world. The only similarities were hardhats and tool belts. Most of these guys and their tools floated in the air. The only members of the crew on ladders or on the ground were shifters and a lone satyr.

A young, muscular man approached us and I recognized him as a member of the werewolf pack, although I didn't remember his name.

"You three just increased the value of this property tenfold," he said, leering at us.

I rolled my eyes. If he wolf whistled, I was out of here.

Astrid grabbed the rim of his yellow hardhat and yanked it down over his face. "I'm the damn sheriff, you fool. Do you want to see a Valkyrie in action? Try disrespecting me again."

The young werewolf flipped up his hardhat and held up his hands, acquiescing. "It was meant as a compliment. My bad."

"Where's your boss?" Astrid asked.

"I'm the foreman here," he said. "Tommy Spinelli."

"Your boss is the owner of this building, not the foreman," Astrid said. "Is she around?"

Tommy shielded his eyes from the glaring sunlight. "She's in the trailer on the other side of the building. She likes to work on site." He lowered his voice. "She's a bit of a control freak, you know? Constantly checking on us."

"Thanks for your help, Tommy," Astrid said.

"Anytime," he said, with a wink. "And I do mean anytime."

Astrid strode toward the trailer and Britta and I hustled behind her. The trailer was the size of a shed and clearly not intended for long-term use. The door was open so Astrid stuck her head inside.

"Mrs. Bogan?" she asked.

"Yes, yes. What is it? Come in."

The three of us crowded into the tiny trailer. Serena Bogan sat behind a desk that was covered in paperwork. She wore a navy blue business suit and a hardhat rested on the edge of the desk.

"Sheriff Astrid," she said, mildly surprised. Serena leaned back in her chair and examined her. "Angels above, it's good to see a non-moron wearing the star badge. Do you think this role will become permanent for you?"

"I appreciate your support, ma'am," Astrid said. "To be honest, I have no idea what the mayor intends. Between you and me, I don't know if she's simply punishing Hugo or if she really intends for me to be the new sheriff."

"From what I hear, the entire town is thrilled to have a competent sheriff for a change. On that note, is there something I can help you with?"

"As a matter of fact, there is," Astrid said. "I understand that you recently had an argument with the building inspector."

"Ed Doyle." Serena's cheeks paled. "Ah, I see where this is going. He's dead now, isn't he? I read about it in the paper."

"If you see where this is going," Astrid said, "then maybe you can help it along by offering your side of the story."

Serena balked. "Oh, I have a side of the story, do I? I suppose I do. I wasn't happy when the building failed the initial inspection. My crew has been working overtime to prepare for the opening. Ed Doyle set us back two more weeks."

"Is that all?" Astrid asked.

Britta elbowed her sister in the ribs. "You know that's not all. She tried to bribe him."

Astrid pursed her lips. "I was getting to that part. Just let me talk, okay?" She returned her focus to Serena. "How much did you offer him to pass inspection?"

Serena folded her arms and glared at us. "I'm not saying a word. I'm not going to be implicated in any crimes. It's bad enough you're questioning me about murder, but you're also trying to put me on the hook for bribing a public official."

"Listen, Mrs. Bogan," I said. "Astrid is being polite because she respects you. If you give her a hard time, she'll have no choice but to make you answer these same questions down at the police station. We all know that you'd much rather be on site, monitoring the construction. It's up to you, though. If you want to waste your time and everyone else's, we can bring you down to the station right now and keep you there indefinitely."

Astrid bit back a smile.

Serena narrowed her eyes at me. "And you are?"

"She's my consultant," Astrid said. "Now that I'm in charge, I prefer a more collaborative approach to law enforcement. It's one of the ways Sheriff Hugo and I differ."

"I've never been a fan of collaboration myself," Serena said. "I find I'm usually the best person to get the job done."

"Even as a shifter?" I asked. I thought all shifters had a pack mentality.

"I'm a wereweasel," Serena said. "We're more self-reliant than other shifters. In my experience, other people just hold me back."

"Other people like Ed Doyle?" I asked.

Serena ran her tongue over her top teeth, assessing me. "It's true that I was unhappy with the results of the inspection."

"So unhappy that you offered to bribe him?" Astrid asked.

"If I answer you honestly, then I don't want to be charged with attempted bribery or any such nonsense," Serena said.

Astrid pressed her fingertips on the edge of the desk and fixed Serena with her hard stare. "It's not up to you to decide. You'll answer my questions honestly because I'm the sheriff and you are a citizen of Spellbound. Got it?"

Serena's shoulders slumped in defeat. "Fine. Yes, I tried to bribe him. No, he refused to accept it. Happy now?"

"Not quite," Astrid said. "Did you kill him?"

"Why would I?" Serena asked. "The damage had been done. He reported me and I failed the inspection. I had nothing to gain from murdering him."

"If he's dead, he can't testify against you in a bribery trial," I said.

"No, but his report could be admitted into evidence," Serena replied. "I'm sure it would be enough for a conviction."

She was probably right. "When was the last time you saw Ed?" I asked.

"In the Spotted Owl," Serena said. "I was there with my construction crew after one of our long workdays. Ed was there with members of his bowling league."

"Did you speak with him that night?" Astrid asked.

"I tried to buy him an ale," she said. "He refused that, too.

He was very concerned with the appearance of impropriety." She shook her head. "Talk about an honorable man. You don't meet many of those."

It made me wonder how many others she'd successfully bribed in town over the years.

"Did he drive his jalopy there?" I asked.

Serena shrugged. "I have no idea. I was a bit tipsy when I left, so I can't say I took much notice of the parking lot."

"How did you get home if you were drunk?" Astrid asked.

Serena's brow lifted. "Why? Would you like to charge me with drunk driving as well?"

"No, but I might want to corroborate your story."

"Fine. Tommy, my foreman, took me home." She pressed a finger to her lips. "But don't tell my husband. He's not a fan of werewolves."

I suspected Mr. Bogan also wasn't a fan of a werewolf boning his wife.

"Did you notice anything unusual at the pub?" I asked. "You said he was with members of his bowling league. Did they seem to be enjoying themselves?"

Serena rubbed her chin. "Now that you mention it. They were in poor spirits. They'd lost a big game and seemed to be commiserating."

"Commiserating or arguing?" Astrid asked.

"I really don't know," Serena replied. "But I recognized a couple of his teammates. Harlan Michaelson and Mitch Gannon. You might want to have a word with them."

"Thanks, we will," Astrid said.

"So you're not dragging me down to the station?" Serena looked relieved.

"Not today," Astrid said. "But we may need you to answer more questions later on."

"It's best to schedule me in after business hours," Serena

said, already forgetting which one of them was actually in charge.

"I'll bear that in mind," Astrid said wryly.

We left the trailer and Astrid glanced at her sister. "What do you think?"

"Maybe she had one of her crew take care of the ladder," Britta suggested.

"Doubtful," I said. "She made it clear that she likes to take matters into her own hands. If she's the culprit, then she's the one who tampered with the ladder."

Astrid eyed me curiously. "But you don't think she did it?"

I shook my head. "Like she said. She had nothing to gain at that point. Ed had filed a report and her building still failed."

Astrid nodded in agreement. "I guess it's time we track down the bowling league."

"I have a better idea," Britta said. "Why don't head over to the Spotted Owl later and talk to them there when their guards are down? A few ales and everybody's a chatty Cathy."

Astrid squeezed her sister's arm. "That's a great idea."

Britta looked shocked. "Really? Because it was only an excuse to drink and ogle hot guys."

"You can do that, too," I said. "Two birds, one stone." Sedgwick hated that expression, which only made me want to use it more.

"Meet there at eight?" Astrid said.

"Absolutely. Mind if I invite a few friends?" I asked. "Make it seem like a legitimate girls' night out."

"The more, the merrier," Astrid said.

I took hesitant steps up the walkway and knocked on Elsa's front door. I knew it was a risk coming here. If she came back too soon and saw me, she might make sure that I took a hike from Daniel's life permanently. Or she might make a more concerted effort to excise me from his life.

I inhaled deeply and tapped on the door.

Are you sure about this? Sedgwick asked.

I poked my head out from under the front porch to see him circling the house above. "What are you doing here? I deliberately didn't tell you where I was going because I didn't want you to follow me.

If you are going to make a spectacular fool of yourself, I don't want to miss it, Sedgwick said.

I stuck out my tongue at him. "Gee, you're such a good friend. What would I ever do without you?"

I returned to the door just as it opened. Daniel stood there in his bare feet, his white wings spread wide behind him. I'd almost forgotten how breathtaking they were up close. The memory flashed in my mind of the feel of those wings when I rode on his back. They were soft, yet so strong. Like Daniel.

"Hi, Emma," he said, looking baffled to see me. "What brings you here?"

"I feel like we haven't seen much of each other since the engagement," I said. "I wanted to see how the wedding plans are coming along."

"Why do you come on in and we can talk about it?" He stepped aside to let me enter.

The house was the same as the last time I'd been inside. Of course, that time I'd been invisible so neither Daniel nor Elsa knew I'd been here with them. Her taste was as stark and cold as she was.

"I heard about your case with the nightshade," Daniel said. "How's that going?"

"They're a tight-knit group," I said. "I think because they are smaller than the werewolves, less information gets out if they don't want it to."

"At least you don't have to defend Fabio," Daniel said with a laugh. "After your date, he'd probably rather go to prison than be defended by you."

"Hey," I exclaimed.

Daniel burst into laughter and it was a glimpse of the Daniel I knew. "Will is a really nice guy. Much too young to take on the responsibility that he has."

"Well, if anyone can help him, I know it's you." As always, his compliment warmed me from the inside out.

"And how's my buddy, Markos?"

My cheeks colored. "You know he's just a friend."

"Like me," he said.

No, not like you, I wanted to scream. Instead, I simply said, "He's incredibly nice. I can see why everyone likes him."

Daniel nodded. "He's had a much more positive impact on the community than I ever have. You should consider him, Emma. He would take good care of you."

My blood began to boil. "No one needs to take care of me. I'm perfectly capable of taking care of myself."

He seemed taken aback. "I didn't mean that you couldn't. Of course I know that you can. You've impressed me from the moment we met. I'm sorry. I didn't mean it that way." He seemed so contrite, I couldn't stay angry.

"Markos is great and he deserves to meet someone really special, but I don't think it's me," I said, calmer now.

Daniel slapped his forehead. "I'm such a terrible host. Can I offer you a drink? A cup of tea?"

My ears perked up at the word tea. "Yes, please. What kind you have?"

He broke into a broad grin. "Elsa makes the best gossamer tea. You need to try it."

I wondered if she kept the tea handy to give it to him in a pinch or if he'd make it from scratch. I watched as he retrieved the teabag from the cabinet.

"I probably won't make it as good as she does," he said. "But I'll do my best."

No, there'd be no magic potion in this one. Doubly lucky for me, although based on what I learned at the academy, since I already had feelings for Daniel, then the potion would have no effect on me.

"I can boil the water if you like," I said.

He slid the mug across the counter to me and I tapped it with my wand. "Double, double, trouble and toil/bring this water to a boil." I watched with satisfaction as tiny bubbles formed and steam Rose from the top.

Daniel gazed at me in wonder. "You're really getting the hang of all this, aren't you?"

"Some days are better than others," I said. In so many ways. "You haven't mentioned anything to Elsa about me, have you?"

He inclined his head. "What about you?" I waited for recognition to set in. "Oh, you mean your secret. No, of course not. I would never do that to you."

I relaxed slightly.

"I think we can trust her, though," Daniel said. "Elsa is so understanding and compassionate. And she loves me. She would never betray me."

I stared into his turquoise eyes. Could he possibly believe the words that were coming out of his mouth?

Daniel backed away from the counter. "What is it? Why are you looking at me like that? Do I have something stuck in my teeth?" He moved to examine his reflection in the window.

"No, don't be silly. I was fascinated by that look of love in your eyes when you spoke of Elsa. It's so charming. She's a lucky fairy."

He returned to the mug and removed the steeped tea bag. "I'm the lucky one," he said. "I feel blessed that she's willing to give me another chance. Considering how badly I messed up last time, it's nothing short of a miracle."

No, the miracle was that Daniel had any feelings for this fairy at all. The glazed look in his eye was unfamiliar to me. I was now more convinced than ever that he was under some sort of spell. It would make sense that it was strongest in the morning. She probably made his tea when he woke up, before she left the house. I had to figure out how many times a day she needed to give it to him to keep him under her spell.

"Would you like any thing in your tea?" he asked. "Honey? I know you like things sweet."

"I really do." Daniel was sweet. It was one of the qualities I liked most about him. Now Elsa was reaping the benefits of it. I hated how jealous I felt. It was an uncommon sensation for me. I tried to think of a time when I'd been jealous before, but nothing came to mind. The closest association I had was the envy I felt when I would see other children with their parents. It wasn't all the time, and it wasn't even necessarily special events. It would strike me at a random moment. I'd be in the grocery store and see a mother looking harried and bent out of shape, chastising her children for probably the fiftieth time that day. Such a normal moment in their lives and I wished for it more than anything. I wished for a mother who scolded me for knocking over the can of beans on the shelf. I would have accepted all of those moments of weakness in exchange for her presence—or my father's—because mixed in with those moments of reprimands were peaceful moments. Loving moments. Riding bikes together. Sharing a cuddle at bedtime. Feeling the unconditional love that came with the parent-child bond.

"So tell me about the wedding plans," I choked out. The words were difficult to say, but I had to be able to continue this friendship if I hoped to save Daniel from Elsa's deceit.

He handed me the steaming mug. "I'm pretty sure my only job is to show up on time. Between Elsa and her mother, I don't get much of a say in anything."

"Does that bother you? It's your wedding too, after all."

"When I raised the point with Elsa, she reminded me that she's very good at organizing and planning. Those are not my strengths."

"How can you say that? You've been organizing and planning your volunteer efforts and doing a great job. The care home has benefited greatly from your organization and planning." He and I were still regulars there, thanks to his philanthropic interests.

"This is a wedding, Emma. My volunteer work is about my redemption. The wedding is a more selfish event. Surely you can see the difference." He moved to the living room. "Why don't we go sit down? But make sure you use a coaster. Elsa doesn't like it when guests ignore the coasters."

I sat across from him in one of the white chairs. She was a brave fairy, having white furniture. I'd never in a million years trust myself not to ruin it. "So when is the wedding? Will it be at the Mayor's Mansion like the engagement party?"

"Elsa wants it at Swan Lake. Invitations will be going out soon. The wedding is set for next month."

"I'm surprised Elsa wants to wait that long," I said.

"She doesn't, but her mother insisted. The mayor's schedule was too busy to accommodate a wedding."

Mayor Knightsbridge was stalling. I still had no idea what she had planned. I wondered whether it was worth bringing my theory to her, or if she'd be resistant to the idea that Elsa was behind this. It was a risk, but it was one I had to take.

"The lake is another reason it's taking longer to plan. Arrangements need to be made for the ceremony to be held there."

"She wants the reception there, too?" I had a hard time imagining a fancy fairy like Elsa Knightsbridge wanting to dine alfresco.

"No, just the ceremony. The reception will be held at the Spellbound Country Club."

Now that made more sense.

"Secretly, I think Mayor Knightsbridge is unhappy at the thought of being a grandmother," he said.

I balked. "Grandmother?" I was pretty sure I'd just popped a blood vessel.

Daniel chuckled. "Not yet. I only meant in the future. Elsa can't wait to be a mother."

My stomach turned. The idea of Elsa and Daniel having children hadn't even occurred to me.

"Is that even possible for you?" I asked.

"Why wouldn't it be? As far as I know, everything is in working order."

A wave of nausea rolled over me. "I'm sorry, Daniel, but the tea isn't settling very well. I think I need to go."

He looked disappointed. At least that was something. "Well, I'm glad you stopped by. We should do this again soon. I miss you."

I couldn't bring myself to look at him. "I miss you, too," I said, and closed the front door behind me.

CHAPTER 14

I USUALLY SOCIALIZED at the Horned Owl, so it felt a bit weird to be sitting in the Spotted Owl for a change. I felt like I was cheating on my pub. The interior was similar, not a surprise since both places were owned by incubi brothers.

"Why do we never come here?" Begonia asked. "It's just as nice as the other one."

"Because of the clientele," Millie said in a hushed tone. "This place is rougher around the edges."

I stifled a laugh. I'd hardly call the patrons here rough around the edges. In fact, I saw the same types of residents that frequented the Horned Owl. There were vampires, shifters, satyrs, nymphs—no group seemed absent from the mix.

"There's Astrid and her sister," Sophie said, waving wildly.

"Sorry we're a little late," Astrid said. "Somebody couldn't find her favorite lipstick and insisted on rifling through my things to make sure I didn't steal it from her."

"I didn't accuse you of stealing," Britta said. "You're the sheriff now. It would look bad."

"It is a pretty shade on you," I said.

"Thanks." Britta beamed at me. "I found it in the kitchen in the cookie jar."

"The cookie jar?" I queried.

Britta waved me off. "Don't ask." She slapped her hands on the table. "Who needs a drink? This round is on me."

All hands went up around the table.

"How about a pitcher of Melon Pizazz?" Begonia suggested.

"Good idea," Britta said. "I'm going to go flirt with the bartender and see if I can get a second pitcher for free."

"No worries about the appearance of impropriety with this one," I whispered to Astrid.

She laughed. "Britta was born improper. Seriously, I think she was breech."

Astrid sat beside me at the table and scanned the room for Mitch or Harlan.

"I wanted to look for them," I said, "but I don't know what they look like."

"I know who they are," Astrid said. "I used to bowl in the same league."

"Really?" I couldn't picture the blond Valkyrie bowling. I pictured the heavy ball sailing through the air and smashing through a window when she felt the urge to celebrate a strike.

"There they are now," she said. "A booth in the back corner. Mitch has the mustache and Harlan is bald."

I craned my neck to see them. Mitch's mustache wasn't as bad as I expected. It was so easy to go wrong with a mustache, but his was more Tom Selleck than Hitler.

"How do we play this?" I asked.

"How about you go over once you have a drink," Astrid suggested. "See if you can get them comfortable and talking. Then I'll swoop in with the questions."

"Sounds good."

"Are you sleuthing?" Begonia asked eagerly. "Can we help?"

"Probably best not to have too many hands in the cauldron," Astrid said.

Begonia fell back against her chair, disappointed.

"There'll be other chances," I said. "There always seems to be a need for sleuthing around here."

Britta arrived with two pitchers and set them in the middle of the table. A server followed with a tray of empty glasses.

"This looks wonderful," I said. I hadn't tried Melon Pizazz yet, although I'd seen other people drinking it on occasion. It reminded me of sangria or some other fruity cocktail. Instead of traditional fruit, there were slices of Spellbound fruit like burstberries and razzle-dazzle.

The server filled the glasses from the pitcher and I took a quick sip.

"What do you think?" Sophie asked.

"So good," I said. "How much alcohol is in here?"

"Enough to knock you off your broom if you're not careful," Millie said. "What am I saying? You don't even ride a broom."

"Thanks for reminding me of my shortcomings, Millie," I said, taking another sip. Like a box of Lucky Charms, it was magically delicious.

"You can always count on me," Millie replied.

"I'm heading over," I said, glass in hand. Before I made it halfway across the room, I was intercepted by a familiar, devastatingly attractive face. "Demetrius."

"Emma," he said, offering me a chaste kiss on the cheek. Who was I kidding? Chaste was impossible for a vampire like Demetrius Hunt. Even his affectionate greetings dripped with sex appeal.

"What are you doing here?" I asked. "Aren't you usually at the Horned Owl?"

"I could say the same to you," he said. "It's Killian's birthday and he prefers this place."

"I didn't realize vampires celebrated birthdays," I said. I hadn't given the matter much thought.

"It's the day he became a vampire," Demetrius clarified. "That's what we celebrate."

I guess that made sense. "Tell him happy birthday for me."

He snaked an arm around my waist. "Why don't you come and tell him yourself? I'm sure everyone will be pleased to see you."

I glanced across the room to where the bowlers were engaged in animated conversation. "Maybe for a minute."

He steered me toward a nearby booth where Killian was nestled between Samson and Edgar. "Look who the hideous thing Gareth called a cat dragged in?"

"Hardy har," I said. "Don't insult Magpie when he's not here to defend himself." And by defend himself, I meant claw their eyes out.

"Happy Birthday, Killian," I said.

"Have a seat," Samson said, moving over to make room on the end for me.

"How's the new boyfriend?" Edgar asked, careful to avoid Demetrius's gaze. I suspected he was warned not to mention Markos.

"I don't have a boyfriend," I said firmly. "Markos is a friend. Just like Demetrius."

"Do you think he has sex in his minotaur form or his human one?" Samson asked.

"I have no idea," I said. "It's not really any of our business, is it?"

"That's the beauty of being a vampire," Edgar said. "We're

sexy in the only form we have. We don't need to disguise our looks."

"If you're going to insult Markos, I'm going to get up now," I said.

Demetrius held out a hand to stop me. "Emma's right. That's enough."

The group fell silent.

"Is it true he had something to do with the building inspector's death?" Killian asked, and quickly realized his faux pas. "Apologies. I'm not trying to besmirch his good name."

"Is that what the rumor mill is saying?" I asked.

Killian nodded. "That's what I heard at the blood bank this morning."

"It's not true," I said. "I mean, the investigation is ongoing, but Markos isn't a suspect."

"That's good news, I guess," Demetrius said.

"Except for the fact that there's a murderer on the loose," Killian said. "Not such good news then."

"Astrid's doing a great job," I said. "She puts her investigations before anything else."

At that moment, a cheer went up across the room. I cringed as Astrid and Britta climbed onto the tabletop and began to dance.

"You were saying?" Killian said pointedly.

"I swear," I said. "She's doing that for a reason, but I can't tell you why." I hoped she was, anyway. I knew the goal was to keep the bowling team relaxed and chatting. If they thought Astrid was drunk, they'd be more likely to talk openly.

"That was quite the engagement party, huh?" Demetrius asked. "I've been to a lot of celebrations, but that one was something else."

"It was something else all right," I said, trying to disguise my bitterness.

"I never thought Daniel would settle," Samson said. "I suppose there's hope for you yet, Dem."

Demetrius's dark eyes met mine. "I'd like to think so."

"Please choose someone less annoying and vain than Elsa Knightsbridge," Edgar said. "If you're going to tether yourself to another being for eternity, she has to be tolerable."

"I'm aiming for a bit more than tolerable," Demetrius said.

"Which is the reason you're still single," Samson said, and everyone laughed. "You need to aim lower, my boy."

"I'd prefer to aim higher." Demetrius brought the bottle of ale to his lips.

"This has been nice catching up," I said. "But I need to go and say hello to someone."

"More friends?" Killian asked. "You've certainly proven to be quite the social butterfly."

I smiled sheepishly. "I like to get to know people." In particular, two bowlers who might know something about a murder. "It was great to see you."

I slid out of the seat and threaded my way through the tables until I reached the back corner booth. At this point, my drink was nearly empty.

"Is this the line for the restroom?" I asked, glancing around in confusion.

Mitch laughed. "There's no line. It's right down that hall." He pointed behind him.

"Thanks." I hesitated. "Nice mustache. Not many men can rock a mustache like that without looking ridiculous."

Mitch straightened in his seat. "Thank you, honey."

I cringed inwardly. I hated when men called me 'honey.' It felt so demeaning. "You look familiar. Haven't I seen you with Ed Doyle?"

Mitch's expression soured. "You knew Ed?"

I nodded. "A shame what happened, isn't it?"

"Terrible," Harlan said. "I'm Harlan Michaelson. We were on Ed's bowling team."

"Oh, I guess that's why I've seen you together," I said.

"Can I get you another drink?" Mitch offered. "What girly cocktail do you have there?"

"A Melon Pizazz," I said, struggling not to clench my teeth. Okay, so maybe it was a girly cocktail, but he didn't have to point it out.

Mitch blew a shrill whistle that got the whole pub's attention. "Another Melon Pizazz for the little lady," he yelled.

I wanted to blend into the furniture. "I heard you guys played an unfortunate game last week."

Harlan groaned. "We shouldn't have lost the championship. It was a sham."

"What happened?" I asked.

"It was Ed…" Mitch hesitated, sensing that perhaps it wasn't wise to speak ill of the dead. "He messed up his last turn. Cost us the championship."

"What do you mean he messed up?" I asked. "What did he do?"

"He had a chance to pick up a spare, which would've given us the win, but he didn't manage it," Mitch said.

"He tripped over his own hooves," Harlan added. "I've never seen Ed trip in his life. He didn't have a clumsy bone in his body."

"So you accused him of throwing the game on purpose?" I asked. My drink arrived and I handed my empty glass to the server.

"I didn't," Harlan said, shooting an accusatory look at Mitch.

"It seems stupid now," Mitch admitted. "I know Ed had no reason to lose."

"You thought he bet against us," Harlan said.

"You guys bet money on the games you play?" I asked.

"Not all of them," Harlan said. "But this was a championship game."

Astrid chose this moment to make her appearance. "Hey, Emma. We've been looking everywhere for you."

"I was making new friends," I said, smiling brightly. "Do you gentlemen know Sheriff Astrid?"

Four heads bobbed.

"Congrats on the promotion," Harlan said. "I hear Hugo's had trouble getting off the sofa these days."

The men at the table laughed loudly.

"He's not happy with me," Astrid said. "That's for sure."

"Why not?" Mitch asked. "It's not your fault he was crap at his job."

"Hugo is a blamer," Harlan said. "He likes to blame others for his inadequacies."

"Sounds like you, Mitch," one of the other guys said.

Mitch glowered at him. "I said I was sorry about blaming Ed. Let's forget it, okay?"

Astrid's ears perked up. "Ed Doyle? You guys knew him, right?"

"We were just telling your friend here about our championship game last week," Harlan said.

"Any idea who murdered him?" Mitch asked. "I guess you must be investigating that."

"I am," Astrid admitted. "I've been talking to people. Is there anyone you can think of? Anyone with a grudge against Ed?"

"Besides Mitch?" Harlan asked, guffawing.

Mitch gave him a sharp jab in the ribs with his elbow. "That's enough, Harlan. It's not funny."

"Because it's true?" Astrid queried.

"I didn't hold a grudge," Mitch insisted. "I was mad for about five minutes."

"Five minutes is long enough to tamper with the rung of a ladder," Astrid said.

Mitch's bushy eyebrows shot up. "Is that what happened? Somebody messed with his ladder?"

Astrid nodded. "It was just weak enough so that when his hoof came down in it, he lost his balance and fell. One of the top rungs was deliberately targeted so that he fell from a good height."

Mitch swallowed hard. "Poor Ed. I gave him such a hard time that night over something so stupid."

Harlan patted him on the back. "Don't beat yourself up. We were all miserable that night. You just more vocal about it."

"Do you think Ed died thinking we hated him?" Mitch asked. I noticed the tears welling in his eyes. I wasn't expecting that reaction.

"Of course not," Harlan said. "He knew how hotheaded we got when things didn't go our way. He wanted that championship too. I bet he blamed himself more than anyone."

"Typical Ed," Mitch said, chugging the rest of his ale. He burped and set the empty mug on the table. "How's that fruity cocktail?"

"It's good," I said. "Would you like to order one?"

"No, I'll just have some of yours." Before I could object, he swiped the drink from my hand and glugged it down. I didn't mind since I had no intention of drinking it after his lips touched the glass. "That's pretty good. What'd you say it's called again?"

"Melon Pizazz," I said.

"I think I'll order a pitcher for the table," he said. "You girls staying?"

Astrid and I exchanged looks.

"I think we need to get back to our friends," I said. "It was nice meeting you."

As we walked back to our table, Astrid nudged me. "Not our guy, huh?"

I shook my head. "I don't think so. Nobody was upset enough to murder Ed. It sounds like it was one drunken night of giving Ed a hard time and then forgotten by morning."

"That was my impression," Astrid agreed. "Thanks for the help."

"Anytime."

"I saw you talking to Demetrius," she said. "Is he still showing his fangs at every opportunity?"

I laughed. "He's made it clear that he's still interested, if that's what you mean."

"It's not my business, but why not give him a try? If you're not interested in Markos and Daniel is marrying Elsa..."

"Daniel is *not* going to marry Elsa," I interjected hotly. I didn't realize how intense my reaction was until I saw the look on Astrid's face. "I'm sorry. I didn't mean to overreact."

"It's okay. I get it. You love him."

Desperately.

"Have you told him yet?" Astrid asked. "Maybe he'd change his mind about Elsa if he knew the truth."

I shook my head. "I...can't do that."

"Why not?"

"Because what if it doesn't matter?" I asked. "What if the information doesn't change his mind?"

Astrid's expression turned somber. "Yeah. There's no good answer, is there?"

I sighed. "I'm afraid not. Kinda like our murder investigation, huh?"

Astrid slung an arm over my shoulder. "You may not get your man, Emma, but, together, we'll get ours."

To say I was nervous about poker night was an understatement. In a short time, I would have enough strong personalities in the house to trigger a third world war. I studied myself in the bathroom mirror, searching for evidence of brain-eating amoebas. That was the only explanation for my agreement to host the Grey sisters *and* the Gorgon sisters at the same event.

"I wouldn't worry about how you look," Gareth said, gliding into the bathroom. "They'll destroy you whether you're pretty or not."

"If I'm going to be turned to stone, I may as well look nice for the rest of eternity," I said, running a brush through my hair.

"No worries," Gareth said. "We'd set you up in the garden. Get a few attractive gnomes to keep you company."

"Hardy har. Very funny." I whirled around, brush in hand. "This is your fault, you know. You begged me to invite them."

"I didn't think you'd actually agree to it," he said. "I expected you to put up more of a fight."

I tossed the brush onto the counter. "Now you tell me."

"If it's any consolation, your hair looks extra shiny this evening."

"It's not, but thanks." I left the bathroom and Gareth followed me closely. If ghosts had the ability to breathe, I'd have felt his warm vampire breath on my neck. "Did you tell Magpie to behave himself? I don't need him tripping anyone and causing a riot."

"He'll be hiding, I imagine," Gareth replied. "You know he doesn't love crowds."

Neither did I and yet I'd invited one to my house. A possible unruly one. What was wrong with me?

"It's good to break out of your comfort zone," Gareth said, as though reading my mind.

I laughed. "Because you're famous for your willingness to deviate from the norm."

He folded his arms. "I don't know what you mean."

I moved to my closet and slid open the door a fraction. "I think I'll leave it like that tonight."

"But...but...Why would you do a thing like that?" Gareth sputtered.

I flashed him an innocent look. "Whatever do you mean? Like what?"

He narrowed his eyes. "Fine. I get the point. Keep it up and you'll get mine." He clicked his fangs together.

"I doubt it," I said. "Lyra would need to be doing a helluva job with your training."

"It will be nice to be seen tonight, if only by a few guests," Gareth mused.

"Tell me the truth," I said. "Is that the real reason you wanted me to invite them? So you'd feel part of the festivities?" On that basis, I was almost willing to forgive him.

"I know they're scary and misunderstood," Gareth said, his head lowered. "But they're better than nothing."

"I'm not nothing," I replied.

"Oh, I didn't mean it that way," he said quickly. "Come on, Emma. You know better than that."

I sighed. "I know. I hope everyone has fun." And I hoped nobody died. The usual poker night aspirations.

The wind chimes sounded and Gareth floated through the front wall to sneak a peek.

"Witches," he said, and I immediately relaxed. I'd asked my friends to come early so that I wasn't alone with Greys and Gorgons.

"Do you want to see if you can open the front door?" I asked.

"Could do," he said. "But they still won't be able to see me."

"They'll know it's you, though." I adjusted my top. "Go on. I'm almost ready."

"Diva," he muttered before disappearing.

I slipped on my shoes and glanced at Sedgwick on his perch. "I thought you had the night off."

And miss this disaster-in-the-making? he asked, his owl eyes rounder than normal. *Not a chance.*

"Try not to get in the way," I said. "If you end up involved in a scuffle, I can't promise to save you."

Same goes for me.

I hurried to the foyer to see Begonia, Sophie, and Millie trying desperately to figure out where Gareth was standing so they could talk to him. Every time one of them turned in the right direction, he'd shift to the side so she was talking to a plant or the wall.

"Gareth, stop that," I admonished him.

He gave me a guilty look before disappearing.

"There you are, Emma," Begonia said, smiling brightly. "Your key looks wonderful on the wall."

I glanced over my shoulder to where the key was proudly mounted and displayed between the large windows. "And it only took two hours to hang with Gareth's overzealous supervision."

"Well, his input paid off," Begonia replied. "So are you ready for the most exciting poker night in the history of Spellbound?"

"Please don't say that," I begged. "I don't want excitement. Fun only." I pointed to the living room. "Visors and chips are on the table."

"Thank the stars," Sophie said. "I'm starving."

"Not those kind of chips," I said. "Poker chips, but there

are snacks in the kitchen. Maybe you can help me carry everything into the living room."

She gave me an embarrassed smile and walked with me to the kitchen. "I was too nervous to eat dinner," she admitted.

"You're not the only one," I said. I was fairly certain the mice in the woods behind the house could hear my stomach growling.

The witches helped me move the snacks and drinks into the living room.

"Why don't we use a spell to do this?" Millie suggested, setting a bottle of lemon fizz on the sideboard.

"Because I need to get rid of this nervous energy," I said. "Keeping busy is the best way to do it."

"Is the nervous energy because of Will's trial tomorrow?" Sophie asked.

"And poker night and Ed Doyle's murder…You name it and I'm nervous about it."

"Shouldn't you be preparing for the trial?" Millie queried.

"I spent hours looking over the file and prepping Will," I said. "Unfortunately, there isn't much more I can do to help him. We have to roll the dice and hope for the best."

The wind chimes sounded and before I had a chance to reach the foyer, Jemima appeared in the doorway. "I heard it was poker night."

I was desperate to roll my eyes, but she was looking straight at me. I was grateful when Gareth materialized behind her and rolled his eyes for me. Jemima was a witch who worked at Mix-n-Match. Her face was as sour as her attitude.

"It's a very special poker night," Begonia said, moving closer to Jemima. "Have you heard about the guests of honor?"

"No," Jemima said. She focused on Begonia, clearly

intrigued. "Who is it? Someone handsome like Demetrius Hunt?"

"No, poker night is for the ladies, remember?" Begonia said.

"Right," Jemima replied. Her brow wrinkled. "It isn't Lady Weatherby, is it? I'd rather not have all the joy sucked out of the room."

Kind of the way we feel when you appear, I said to myself.

"You know what?" Millie said, munching on a handful of sparklecorn. "Let's leave it a surprise. It'll be more fun that way."

"Good idea," Jemima said. "You don't want it to be boring like your remedial classes. I mean, those lessons are designed for idiots."

I balled my fists at my side and resisted the urge to throttle her.

The wind chimes sounded again and I brushed past Jemima at breakneck speed to answer the door. Anything to put a safe distance between us.

The hiss of snakes alerted me to the arrival of the Gorgon sisters. Althea stood front and center, carrying a purple orchid.

"Something new for you to kill," she said, and handed over the pretty flower.

"Seems fairly irresponsible to give her a flower you know she'll murder," Miranda, the eldest Gorgon, said.

I admired the orchid. "I tend to kill the easy ones, but the difficult ones thrive," I said.

"Sounds about right," Gareth muttered under his breath.

"What was that?" I asked.

"Tell Althea she looks lovely tonight," he said clearly.

"Gareth says you look a little top heavy." I pointed to her white turban.

"Monster," he hissed.

"Tell Gareth if he weren't already dead, I'd kill him myself," Althea said, zeroing in on his location.

Gareth backed away slowly. "It's like she can see into my soul."

"You don't have a soul," I reminded him.

"Details, details."

"Come in, ladies. Some eager poker players have already arrived." I held out the flower. "Gareth, do you think you can carry this safely into the kitchen?"

He studied the small pot. "I think I might be able to do that." He inclined his head. "Do you trust me?"

I let go of the pot. To everyone else, it seemed to float in mid-air.

"Amazing," Althea breathed. "This is from working with the Grey sister?"

"Yes. Lyra," I said, and watched Gareth and the orchid disappear into the kitchen. "As a matter of fact…" I didn't have time to finish my sentence before the door swung open and the three Grey sisters stood shoulder to shoulder in the entryway.

"Gorgon cousins," Effie, the taller one, said.

"Grey cousins," Amanda exclaimed. Her snakes began poking their heads outside of her turban for a good look at their long lost relatives.

Oh no.

The six women stared at each other for one long, uncomfortable moment. Then I was quickly shoved aside as they greeted one another in a dizzying fit of arms and lips.

"Your eyes," Amanda said in amazement. "There are two of them."

"The better to see you with, my dear," Lyra said.

"And your teeth are incredible," Miranda said.

"The better to eat you with, my dear," Lyra said, continuing the joke.

Althea glanced at Effie and Petra, the shorter sister, still sharing an eye between them and sporting a single tooth. "When will it be your turn for a makeover?"

"When we earn it," Effie said, nodding toward me. "We wouldn't dare try to outwit our new patron." I heard the words that were unspoken—our new patron, the powerful sorceress full of darkness. Thankfully, no one else filled in the blanks.

I clapped my hands together. "Now that you've had a chance to get reacquainted, why don't you join the other guests in the living room?"

"Who's still missing?" Gareth asked, returning to the foyer.

"Astrid and Britta," I said. "Lucy has a date."

"No harpies?" he queried.

"Not tonight," I said. "I thought it was best to keep it simple."

He chuckled. "Yes, that's how I'd describe tonight. Simple."

"Again, I'd like to remind you that this was your idea."

"I have a feeling you'll be reminding me of this for the rest of your natural life."

"And maybe even after that," I added. Before I could retreat to the living room, Astrid and Britta arrived. They'd clearly been arguing as evidenced by their sullen expressions.

"Everything okay?" I asked.

"It is now," Britta said. "Point me to the booze."

"A Valkyrie after my own heart," a voice said. Petra Grey emerged from the living room, clutching a bottle in her bony fingers.

Britta stared at the single-eyed, nearly toothless woman. "Smoke and bone. I thought you were just a legend."

"And I thought you were just a legend, my lovely," the

Grey sister shot back. "I'm sure we have stories to share." She beckoned the Valkyrie forward.

"Go on, Britta," Astrid prodded. "Don't insult her."

"What's your poison?" Britta asked, joining her at the hip.

"Hemlock," Petra replied.

"No, I mean your drink of choice."

The Grey sister cackled and I watched them head into the kitchen, engrossed in conversation.

"This is weird," I said.

Astrid cast a sidelong glance at me. "*This* is weird? It seems to me your whole life became weird inside of a day."

"Point taken. Let's go play some poker," I said. "And try not to die."

CHAPTER 15

WHEN WILL and I stepped into the Great Hall the next morning, I was surprised to see an unfamiliar woman seated in Rochester's place. So far the wizard was the only prosecutor I'd dealt with and it was my understanding that he was handling Will's case.

I shot a quizzical look at the woman. Her pointy ears and lack of wings told me she was an elf. "Where's Rochester?"

"He came down with a bad bout of food poisoning, I'm afraid," she said. "I'm Sara Santora and I'll be handling this case."

"Have you had time to review the file?" I asked. "Maybe we should ask to postpone."

Sara gave me a reassuring smile. "I've been working alongside Rochester for years. He didn't think I would have any trouble taking this on today."

I trusted Rochester's judgment. If anything, Sara's lack of preparation would be good for my client.

I took my seat beside Will. His olive complexion was beginning to turn a deeper shade of green.

"Are you nervous?" I asked.

His eyes grew round. "Wouldn't you be?"

Definitely. In fact, I would have already thrown up twice in the ladies room before I made it to my seat. Maybe I should have given Will a dose of anti-anxiety potion before we arrived.

The bailiff appeared and announced the arrival of the judge. Today we were fortunate enough to have Judge Lee Melville. He was a taller dwarf, with a thick, silver helmet of hair and his nose reminded me of a triangle with rounded edges.

"Good morning, counselors," he greeted us. "Good morning Mr. Heath. This seems like a cut and dry matter, so hopefully we can finish in less than an hour."

Will shrank in his chair and I jabbed him with my elbow. He immediately straightened.

"Ms. Santora, would you like to start?" the judge said.

Sara stood. "The prosecution would like to call Mr. William Heath to the stand," Sara said.

The judge scratched his head. "What? No introduction today?"

"As you said, Your Honor. It's a simple case. I think a brief conversation with the defendant will suffice."

The judge nodded and motioned for Will to take the stand. As similar as many things were in Spellbound, the differences were in the details. It seemed odd that a system with such severe penalties would be so flexible at the trial stage. It was one of the key reasons I wanted to see reform in the sentencing guidelines. I didn't trust the procedure to reach the right outcome.

I nudged Will. "Go ahead. You'll be fine."

He hesitated before moving his feet and crossing the room to the witness stand.

Sara smiled, trying to put him at ease, and I instantly

warmed to her. "Can you please state your name for the court?"

"William Heath." He began to fidget in his seat. I gave a quick shake of my head to remind him to sit still.

"Is it true, Mr. Heath, that you were arrested in Mix-n-Match in possession of nightshade?"

"Yes, ma'am. It is true."

"And is it further true that no one placed the nightshade in your pocket without your knowledge?" Sara continued.

"No one put the nightshade in my pocket. I took it and out it in my pocket. Nobody else was involved."

Sara smiled at the judge. "No further questions, Your Honor."

Sara returned to her seat and the judge nodded to me. "Miss Hart. Any questions for your client?"

I crossed the room to stand in front of Will. "Did you intend to use the nightshade for any malevolent purpose?"

Will shook his head, "I told you before. My intentions were good."

The judge's brow furrowed. "Excuse me, young man. What do you mean that your intentions were good? You had a deadly plant in your possession."

Before Will could respond, the double doors burst open.

"Stop the trial," a deep voice rumbled. The statement was followed by a loud hacking cough.

"Grandpa," Will exclaimed. "What are you doing here? You should be in bed."

The judge banged the gavel. "Quiet, please." He turned his attention to Atlas. "What is the meaning of this interruption, sir?"

I realized that Atlas wasn't walking in unaided. Anthony Shoostack held him under one arm and the redhead from Anthony's house gripped the other arm. They moved him to the nearest seat and I noticed that

Atlas clutched a white handkerchief. I could see the blood-stains from where I sat.

"My grandson isn't telling you the truth," Atlas said between coughs.

The judge peered at Will. "Is this true, Mr. Heath?"

"No, I'm telling you the truth," Will insisted.

The judge looked back at Atlas. "Are you saying that this boy did, in fact, have a malevolent purpose for possession of the nightshade?"

"I'm saying nothing of the kind," Atlas said hotly. "He got it for me. I asked him to do it." He began to cough again and covered his mouth with the handkerchief. "In actual fact, I begged him. He didn't want to get it. Tried to talk me out of it a dozen times before I threatened to hit him with my cane."

"And where did you obtain this nightshade, Mr. Heath?" the judge asked.

"He didn't steal it from nobody," Atlas said. "I know a place where it grows naturally. I passed it many times in my travels in lion form, back when I was more mobile. I told him exactly where he could find it."

Judge Melville eyed Will. "Still true?"

Will glanced at me hesitantly.

"You need to be honest, Will," I said.

"Yeah, it's true. I didn't steal it from anyone. I followed his instructions and found it on my own."

"Why were you carrying it around town in your pocket?" the judge asked. "Why not just bring it straight to your grandfather?"

"Because he needed something else to mix with it," Atlas interjected. "I wanted to make sure the job got done right."

The judge's face hardened. "And what exactly did you intend to do with this nightshade mixture?"

Atlas wiped his mouth with a handkerchief. "I wanted him to kill me. I wanted that cocktail to be toxic enough so that I never had to cough again. So that I was no longer a burden to my family. I couldn't get any of it myself, not in my current condition."

The room fell silent. So Atlas had asked his grandson to make a death potion. He had asked twenty-year-old Will to euthanize him. My stomach clenched at the thought. Poor Will.

The judge addressed Will again. "Did you know what your grandfather intended?"

"Yes, sir. I tried to talk him out of it, but he was insistent. He's been sick for a long time, you see."

"What about other means of easing this suffering?" Judge Melville asked. "Have you been to see a healer? There are lots of things…"

"No more healers," Atlas said adamantly, kicking off another coughing fit.

"My grandfather has been visited by many healers over the last few years," Will said. "Nothing has worked. He's in a lot of pain. The coughing hurts his whole body and wears him out."

"It would be a mercy," Atlas said. "My grandson is a good boy. A brave boy who looks after his family."

"What kept you from coming forward until now?" the judge asked Atlas.

"I didn't even know he'd been arrested until recently," Atlas said. "Will made sure that the news was kept from me. I only found out about the trial an hour ago."

"I knew he would get himself in trouble to get me out of trouble," Will explained. "He's too sick to go to prison. He'd suffer more there."

"Well, I don't know that he would have gone to prison," the judge said. "After all, you're still the one who obtained the nightshade, not your grandfather."

Atlas tried to stand, but Anthony kept still. "I'm the one

who told him to get it. Don't you understand? He only got it because I told him to, because he respects his elders. That's a good boy there."

"And he's quite lucky that he was found before he actually gave you a death potion," the judge said. "Otherwise we might be sitting here discussing a murder charge and you wouldn't be here to defend him."

Will looked like he was ready to burst into tears.

"Your Honor," I said. "I think we've established that Will is a good citizen of Spellbound and that he is respectful and committed and kind. Maybe we can think about assigning him a year of community service."

The judge rubbed his chin thoughtfully. "Mr. Shoostack, you are the alpha of the werelion pride. What do you have to say for your cub?"

Anthony rose to his feet. "I would simply echo what Atlas said. Will Heath is the best example of a werelion. He embodies all of the best qualities we have to offer. His loyalty is what has him sitting here now. The practical outcome is that if Will goes to prison, he will leave behind his grandfather, his mother, and two minor siblings. The family would suffer greatly."

The judge looked at Sara. "Any strong feelings on the matter, counselor?"

"I don't think we should lose sight of the fact that euthanasia is against the law in Spellbound," Sara said. "If Will had gone ahead and fixed the death potion and served it to his grandfather, he would absolutely be facing a murder charge."

My blood pressure began to rise. I was hoping Sara would show compassion for young Will.

"That being said," she continued, "we are fortunate enough to have the testimony of his grandfather. Some of you know my grandfather, Fagan. If he asked me to do the same, I don't know that I would have refused him." She surveyed the room. "It's a difficult and terrible situation and my heart goes out to Will's family."

"I would have taken the death potion myself," Atlas said. "I wouldn't have had Will feed it to me."

"But he still would've been the one to gather the ingredients and make the potion," the judge said. "The fact that he didn't bring it to your lips is neither here nor there."

Atlas slumped in his chair. The full realization of his actions sinking in.

"Have you ever considered moving to the Spellbound Care Home?" I asked. The staff cared for many sick and elderly residents. They'd probably do a better job than what Will was managing to do. Plus it would ease the burden on Will.

"We take care of our own," Anthony said.

"Not this time, it seems," the judge said, not unkindly. "I'm sure you've done your best, but sometimes we need to know when to let go."

"I know some people there," I said. "I can arrange a meeting if you're interested." Although they couldn't cure him., I knew that they would be at least able to make him more comfortable.

Atlas gave a gruff nod.

The judge focused on Will. "Why don't you return to your seat and I'll render the verdict?"

As usual, Will obeyed his elders and joined me at the table.

"Under these unusual circumstances," Judge Melville began, "I sentence you, William Heath, to one year of community service, the service itself to be determined by your pride leader." He banged the gavel. "Case dismissed."

Will blinked. "That's it?"

I smiled. "That's it."

He stared into space, still uncertain. "I can go?"

"Yes, you can go." He ran to his grandfather and the two werelions embraced. I felt the sting of tears in my eyes.

"It was the right outcome," Sara said. "Judge Melville is sensible, thank the gods."

"That's been my experience so far," I said.

"Rochester has been talking about your efforts to amend the sentencing guidelines," Sara said. "Any chance I can get on that committee?"

"Once it gets approved," I said. "You'd be more than welcome."

"Great." She extended a hand. "You're a persistent witch. We need more residents like that in town. Change only happens if people are willing to put in the work."

My heart tightened in my chest as her words hit home. I had to put in the work if I expected anything to change.

"I couldn't agree more," I said. "Now if you'll excuse me, there's somewhere I need to be."

CHAPTER 16

I STRODE up the steps to the oversized doors of the Mayor's Mansion. Lucy was surprised to see me when I appeared in the foyer.

"Hey, Emma. Do you have an appointment with the mayor?" She tapped her dimpled cheek. "I'm pretty sure I would remember if you were on the calendar."

"It's an informal visit," I said. "Is she available? I only need a few minutes."

Lucy shot me a quizzical look. "She is. She's reviewing the minutes from the last council meeting. She always signs off on them once she's reviewed them. I'll let her know you're here."

"Thanks." I appreciated that she was the kind of friend who didn't press me for more information than I was willing to give.

I only had to wait two minutes before Lucy fluttered back to the foyer. "She said she's glad you're here."

Well, that was a start.

"How was your date the other night?" I asked, as I followed Lucy down the long corridor to the mayor's office.

Lucy grimaced. "Don't ask. Back to the drawing board."

"That's too bad."

"You're telling me. I'm going to catch warts from all the frogs I've been kissing. Where's my prince already?"

I laughed. "Hang in there, Lucy. You'll meet him sooner or later."

"Easy for you to say," Lucy began, and then faltered. "I guess it isn't easy for you to say. Sorry."

I waved her off. "It's okay. Really."

Mayor Knightsbridge sat behind her large desk, quill in hand. She set it down when I entered, prepared to give me her full attention.

"Thank you, Lucy," she said. "You may leave us now."

Lucy's confused expression told me that this was an unusual request. Nevertheless, she complied without protest. Once she closed the door behind her, Mayor Knightsbridge gestured for me to sit.

"This might be a long conversation," the mayor said. "Do yourself a favor and get comfortable."

"I guess you know why I'm here," I said.

"The wedding is a month away," she said. "If you didn't come to see me this week, I was planning to come and see you."

"Daniel told me that you're the reason it's a month away. That you managed to delay it." I leaned forward. "So what's your plan?"

She shrugged. "My plan was to stall the big event until I came up with a better plan. What's yours?"

I laughed. "You're the politician. Surely you can come up with a good strategy to stop a wedding. Is there anything bureaucratic we can do?" Spellbound was rife with red tape. "Any rules on the books that prevents an angel from marrying a fairy?" I cringed the moment the words left my mouth. The idea was downright racist.

"No, no," she said. "Interspecies relationships are common here and quite acceptable."

Heat rose to the back of my neck. I was ashamed of myself for even thinking it. I was more desperate than I realized.

"Daniel says that Elsa really wants children. What if Daniel couldn't have children? Is it possible to make them believe that?"

Mayor Knightsbridge suppressed a smile. "Why Miss Emma Hart. You are more devious and diabolical than I imagined. I have to admit that I'm a little in awe of you right now."

I wasn't in awe of me. In fact, I felt desperate for a shower. This wasn't the way to win Daniel. I was stooping to Elsa's level. If I was willing to compromise my fundamental values to win him, then maybe I didn't deserve him after all.

"Forget that idea," I said. "I think there's a more straightforward approach."

The mayor looked intrigued. "And what's that?"

I had to tell her my theory about the Obsession spell. Even though it implicated Elsa, her mother was the one person who would want to see it undone.

"I think Daniel may be under some kind of Obsession spell," I said. "If we can figure out exactly what it is, then maybe we can break it."

The mayor stared at me briefly before exploding in a fit of laughter. "Emma, you sweet thing. It doesn't take much for a man to fall head over heels for my daughter. She is extraordinarily beautiful."

"Yes, but this is *Daniel*," I said.

"Yes, and he fell in love with her once before. Why not twice?"

Because I know him better than anyone, I wanted to tell her. *He wasn't in love with her then and he isn't in love with her now.*

"Then I guess desperate times call for desperate measures," I said.

Mayor Knightsbridge lifted a pale eyebrow. "What does that mean?"

"I'm seeing him tonight at the care home. I think it's time I tell him how I feel."

Mayor Knightsbridge pressed her pink lips together. "That's your plan? Throw yourself at his feet?"

I shrugged. "At this point, honesty is the only weapon I've got."

"This is similar to a game called Pictionary that we play in the human world," I said. The residents of the Spellbound Care Home stared at me, clueless as to what Pictionary was. "The team that's up nominates one person to draw and the other members of the team have to guess what the phrase or title is from the images."

"Where do we get the phrase or title?" Estella asked.

"They're written on slips of paper here," I said, patting my pocket. "I'll hand one out at the beginning of each round."

"What's the phrase or title from?" Minerva asked. She was an elf who lived down the hall from Estella.

"A book or movie," I said. "Or a commonly used phrase. Like spell's bells."

"There are seven of us," Silas said. "Don't we need even numbers if we're in two teams?"

"My team will take the Halo Hottie," Agnes said, winking suggestively at Daniel.

"I'm afraid I'm spoken for," Daniel said.

Agnes's expression darkened. "Yes, I heard that dreadful bit of news. I thought perhaps it was just idle gossip."

My stomach twisted into knots. I was dreading my conversation with Daniel later this evening.

"Now Agnes," Daniel said. "You know I'm very fond of you, but our relationship was never going to progress beyond friendship."

I wondered if he was being deliberately obtuse or if he really thought that Agnes was referring to herself as the disappointed party. She was a wily old witch, and I had no doubt that she recognized my feelings for Daniel based solely on our visits here.

"Let's get started," I said. I didn't want the conversation to take an unexpected turn toward me. It was bad enough being on the receiving end of sympathetic looks from my friends. I didn't need to encounter it at the care home as well. In some ways, this place had become a safe haven. It was cut off enough from town to provide me with a little space and also a little quiet time with Daniel. This seemed to be the one place where we were more like ourselves. Even this evening when we were setting up in the cafeteria, there were a few brief and glorious moments where I forgot all about Elsa and the wedding.

"Well, I'm not playing if the teams are uneven," Silas moaned, folding his arms across his chest. "It's inherently unfair."

Daniel gave an exasperated sigh. "Fine. I'll be on a team."

"Not you," Silas said. "I want Emma on our team. You can be the moderator."

I bit back a smile and handed the scraps of paper to Daniel.

"You draw first, Emma," Estella said. "Show us how it's done."

"I'm not much of an artist," I said. "I'll do my best, though."

"Isn't that the point?" Agnes asked. "Aren't we supposed to laugh at each other's crude drawings?"

"Sometimes that happens," I said. And it would definitely happen now. I was terrible at drawing. More often than not, my art teachers believed I was trying to be funny when I turned in a piece of artwork. Usually it was no better than a toddler's handiwork.

Daniel held out the scraps of paper and I chose one. Cinderella. Okay, I was fairly certain everyone in the room was familiar with the fairytale. Pop culture references were often difficult, but traditional folklore and fairytales were common knowledge here.

My team consisted of Agnes, Estella, and Silas. I tried to think about which element would be the most obvious to them. A pumpkin seemed simplest. As I began to draw, I queried whether the pumpkin was only in the Disney version. Was there one in the original French tale? Crap on a stick, I wasn't sure.

"What is that?" Agnes asked, squinting.

"I'm pretty sure that's the point of the game," one of the members of the other team said—a wizard named Donald.

Agnes glared at him. "Yes, I understand the rules. Thank you, Donald. But what she's drawn doesn't even look like a shape known to man."

I stepped back to study my attempt at a pumpkin. It wasn't quite round enough to qualify. More like a square pumpkin with rounded edges. And now I was pretty sure there was no pumpkin in the French version.

"Hold on," I said. I scribbled over the pathetic shape and tried again. I drew a girl in plain clothes in front of a fireplace. Below that picture, I drew a girl in a ball gown. Then I drew an arrow from the top picture to the bottom one.

Estella frowned. "Are those people or cats?"

"She can't answer that," Daniel said. He scratched his chin. "To be honest, though, I'm not sure myself."

"Traitor," I hissed.

I saw the hint of a smile on his lips. There was my Daniel. I glanced at the clock and realized it was nearly eight o'clock.

I wondered whether the Obsession potion was wearing off. Maybe that was the reason I tended to see glimpses of the Daniel I knew in the evening.

"Can we use magic?" Silas asked.

I placed a hand on my hip. "You're banned from using magic in the care home, so what do you think?"

Silas fell silent.

"No amount of magic can help that anyway," Agnes said, pointing to my drawing.

"Hey," I objected. "You wanted me on your team."

"Technically he did," Agnes said. "And that's only because he can see down your shirt when you bend forward to draw."

I shot a quick look at Silas, who flashed me a guilty grin. "You can't deny an old man the few pleasures he has left."

"Well, I sure can," Agnes said, glaring at him.

"Agnes, my sweet," he cooed. "Try as you might, you deny me nothing."

Agnes shook a bony finger at him. "I'm going to deny ever knowing you if you don't shut up right now."

He grabbed her finger and kissed the tip of it.

"Can we get back to the game?" Estella asked. "I'm feeling nauseous watching the two of you."

We played three rounds before their energy flagged, which suited me fine because I was exhausted from a long day.

"Goodnight, my angel," Agnes said, blowing Daniel a kiss.

"Take care, Agnes," he said. "See you next time."

"Wear tighter pants," Agnes said. "I can't quite admire the curve of your butt in these."

"I'll try to remember," he said, suppressing a smile.

Once the participating residents retired to their rooms for the evening, Daniel and I set to work tidying up the cafeteria. He swept up the debris while I put away the drawing board and other game paraphernalia.

"I think we'll see a care home wedding before too long," he said, in that good-natured tone that I'd grown to adore. It was a far cry from the brooding angel I'd first met. He'd become less Eeyore, more Tigger. Okay, not quite as excitable as Tigger. Maybe more Winnie the Pooh.

"It won't be Agnes and Silas, if that's what you think," I said. "I don't think it's that kind of relationship."

"No?" He seemed genuinely perplexed. "They seem like a perfect match."

"I think they enjoy each other's company, but I don't see Agnes willing to commit." Or Silas, for that matter. The genie liked to pursue the ladies.

"That's too bad. I'd enjoy attending a wedding. It would be nice to celebrate that type of happiness."

A lump formed in my throat. "You'll be attending your own soon enough," I said. "Never mind someone else's."

"That's true," he mused. "I suppose my own wedding will be the height of happiness."

I strangled a scream, but not before a high-pitched sound escaped my lips.

He glanced at me quizzically. "You sound funny. Is something wrong?"

I cleared my throat and busied myself with a container of markers. "No, of course not. What could be wrong?" My palms began to sweat. I didn't think I could go through with my confession. It was too hard. I wasn't ready to take the risk.

"I get the impression that you're unhappy about the wedding."

I took a particular interest in the black marker in my hand. I debated whether I could stab myself in the eye with it and end this conversation.

"Emma." Daniel's fingers encircled my wrists and the

marker clattered to the floor. "You're supposed to be my best friend. You can tell me anything."

"That's just it, isn't it?" I said.

He gave me a blank look. "What?"

"I can't be your best friend," I said. "That role rightfully belongs to your fiancée." I wanted to squirm out of his grip, but part of me refused to budge. I liked the feel of his hands on mine far too much to jerk away.

"It isn't like that with Elsa," he said. "Our relationship is...different."

I gazed into those mesmerizing turquoise eyes, my confidence building. "But should it be different? I mean, don't you want to marry your best friend?"

He appeared genuinely confused. "So are you telling me you aren't looking forward to the wedding?"

"No, Daniel. I'm not." I gulped, recognizing the moment of truth was here. I had to speak now or forever hold my peace. "The truth is Daniel—I don't want you to marry Elsa."

"Why not?" he asked. "Don't you like her? I know she can be a bit much, but if you give her a chance…"

"I could never like her, Daniel," I said. "Not with all the chances in the world."

"Why not?"

"Because she has the one thing in the world I've ever wanted."

"What's that—beautiful blond hair? A perfect nose? Because I'm sure you can do a spell for that."

"No spell," I choked out. "It's nothing so superficial."

"Then what is it?"

"You, Daniel. She has you."

Daniel blinked. He was so quiet for a moment, I thought maybe he hadn't heard me.

"Me," he repeated softly.

"You." My heart pounded so hard, it felt like a wrecking

ball inside my chest. If I didn't end this soon, I was going to be sick.

"Are you sure?" he asked.

"Am I sure? What kind of question is that?" Did he think I didn't know my own heart?

"Maybe you only think you want me," he said.

"I don't just want you, Daniel. I love you. I love you like I've never loved anyone in my life. When I'm with you, I feel like the sun is shining on me." And when he wasn't with me, the world seemed cold and dark. "I wrap my feelings for you around me like a warm blanket on a cold night."

Daniel stared at me like he'd never seen me before. "Are you sure?"

I wanted to smack his beautiful angelic face. "Stop asking me that. Of course I'm sure."

His vacant expression only served to remind me of the spell he was under. So much for true love breaking the spell. Then it occurred to me. It wasn't simply true love. It was true love's kiss. On a whim, I grabbed his cheeks and pulled him toward me, planting a firm kiss on his lips. I stood back and watched him.

"Anything different?" I asked.

His brow creased. "Why? Should there be? Why did you kiss me? You know I'm engaged to Elsa."

My heart sank. "You don't feel anything for me?"

"I...I care about you," he said, looking perplexed. "Whenever I think of you, though, an image of Elsa pops into my head. It's...confusing."

There was no getting through to him unless I could stop Elsa from giving him the potion. Short of hiding in her house, I wasn't sure how to achieve that.

"You'll still come to the wedding, won't you?" he asked. "It won't be the same without you there."

I closed my eyes, trying to keep the tears at bay. "Of course, Daniel. Anything for you."

"I know it's not my place, but I'd rather see you there with Markos than Demetrius."

"It's a month away," I said. "A lot can happen in a month." Like Daniel getting engaged to a cold and calculating fairy.

"Do you want me to fly you home?" he asked.

"No thanks. I've got Sigmund."

He smiled. "Do you remember when I had him fixed up for you? You were so pleased. Your grandmother's old car."

My chest felt like it was going to explode. "I remember, Daniel. I remember every nice thing you've ever done for me."

"Because you love me?"

I nodded sadly. "Because I love you."

CHAPTER 17

WE SAT in the secret lair, watching *Love, Actually*. I'd probably seen it a hundred times, but I never tired of watching it.

"Did you ever notice that the older women in the movie are the only two characters who don't get happy endings?" Laurel asked. "What does that say about how older women are viewed in the human world?"

"It isn't only older women who don't get happy endings," I said glumly.

Sophie gave my arm an affectionate squeeze. "It'll all work out in the end."

"Will it?" I wasn't so sure.

Millie sat in the corner with the voodoo dolls, plucking Lady Weatherby's antlers with her fingers.

"What's the problem, Millie?" Sophie asked.

Millie glowered. "Lady Weatherby told me she was disappointed in my wandwork yesterday. As far as I'm concerned, there was nothing wrong with it. She's picking on me for no good reason."

"She is known for her high standards," I said sympathetically. "Think of it this way. You're still her star pupil."

"That's not saying much in this group," Millie grumbled.

Begonia clutched her heart. "Ouch."

"I feel like I'll be a remedial witch forever," Millie complained. "It isn't fair. I do so many spells better than witches who've already graduated from the academy. You should see Jemima try to do a simple glamour. I run circles around her, yet she's the one working in Mix-n-Match."

I agreed that it did seem unfair that someone like Jemima could scrape by with low marks in every subject, while Millie simply failed to show an aptitude for a minor few. A plan began to take shape in my mind.

"If you want to prove yourself, I have an idea that might help," I said.

Millie gave me a suspicious look. "Like what?"

"Remember that invisibility spell that Felix performed on me?" When he realized that I was close to uncovering his identity as the person who cast a youth spell on the town council, he cast a spell on me to make me invisible. If I had stayed that way for too long, I simply would have faded from the physical world forever.

"What about it?" Millie asked. "That's a really advanced spell."

I smiled. "Exactly. Maybe if you could show Lady Weatherby that you're capable of performing a complex spell like that, she might be more willing to overlook your inadequacies."

"It doesn't work that way," Laurel said. "We have to pass every class or we have to repeat them all. It doesn't matter how well Millie flies a broom or performs an advanced spell, if she can't pass them all, then she can't graduate from the remedial class."

As much as I loved Laurel, I fervently wished she weren't here right now. I needed Millie's help in order for this plan to work. I wasn't sure that I could perform the spell on myself. It was best to have help.

Millie scratched at the eyes of the Lady Weatherby doll. "Why do you want me to perform an invisibility spell anyway?"

"Because I need to be invisible again," I said.

The other girls immediately objected. I heard a chorus of 'are you mad?' and 'spell's bells.'

"It's the only way I can sneak into Elsa's house again and figure out what she's done to Daniel. There must be evidence of an Obsession potion somewhere in the house."

The other girls exchanged wary glances.

"What is it?" I asked. "Is there something you're not telling me?"

Laurel drew a breath. "We're worried about you. We know it's been hard for you to see Daniel with someone else. Just because life doesn't go your way, though, that doesn't mean there's a spell responsible for it."

"We're sure it must seem that way to you," Sophie said. "Under the circumstances, that's been your experience in Spellbound. A spell happened long ago and you're paying the price for it now. But that doesn't mean that every bad thing that happens to you is down to a spell."

I stared at my friends in disbelief. Did they really think it was possible that Daniel truly loved Elsa? That I was being paranoid and delusional?

"There's one flaw in your logic," I said. "I don't consider being trapped in Spellbound to be a bad thing or a problem." At least not anymore. "In fact, getting stuck here is probably the best thing that's ever happened to me. It brought me to you." And to Gareth, Althea, and countless others. And Daniel, of course. Always Daniel.

Begonia chewed her lip thoughtfully. "Maybe we should

help her. If nothing else, it will at least prove one way or another whether Daniel's feelings for Elsa are genuine."

I reached for her hand and squeezed it. "Begonia, you probably know better than anyone that Daniel and I have a special connection. You've seen it firsthand. Do you honestly believe that he woke up one day and forgot about me? That those feelings simply vanished?"

"But it's been *your* feelings we were sure about," Begonia said. "Daniel's feelings were unclear. I mean, that's the whole reason you didn't confess your love for him, right? Because you were afraid that he felt only friendship for you. When you think about it that way, it isn't so crazy to think that he's engaged to Elsa."

She had a point. And it made me want to disappear into a dark hole and never see sunlight again.

I slumped against the back of the sofa. I didn't love the idea of handling this by myself, but if that was what I had to do...

Millie returned the voodoo doll to the wicker basket. "I'll help you," she said.

My head jerked toward her. "You will?"

"You will?" the other girls chorused.

"Like Begonia said, it's the only way to know for sure. And, selfishly, I'd like to see if I can manage the spell."

I rushed forward and threw my arms around her. "Thank you, Millie. This means the world to me."

"Then I'll help," Begonia said. "Someone needs to make sure we can make her visible again. That will be my job."

Sophie glanced around the room hesitantly. "I'm in. If one of us is going to get in trouble, we may as well *all* get in trouble."

I looked at Laurel. "You don't have to join in. I understand if you don't want any black marks against you."

"Are you kidding?" Laurel asked. "Part of me hopes you're

right, Emma. I don't want to see him marry Elsa any more than you do. If he hitches his wagon to an awful fairy like her, he'll never get his halo restored."

"And I desperately want Emma to have her HEA," Begonia said, sighing dramatically.

"HEA?" I queried.

"Happily Ever After," Begonia said incredulously.

"I didn't realize it had its own acronym." As much as I liked the idea of it, I wasn't sure I was lucky enough to have an HEA of my own. Such endings were usually reserved for singing princesses and girls with gorgeous hair. Sadly, I was neither.

"No matter what happens, we're on your side, Emma," Sophie said. "Whatever you want, we want it for you. That's what friends are for."

Feeling overwhelmed, I hugged my knees to my chest. "Thanks. You have no idea how much it means to me to hear you say that." And it was my life's goal to be the kind of person who deserved their friendship. No matter what happened.

CHAPTER 18

I AWOKE EARLY the next morning feeling slightly better than I did the day before. It helped to know that my friends were willing to assist me, although deep down I feared there was a hole in my heart that would never be filled.

Quietly I opened the bedroom door so as not to disturb Sedgwick and Magpie. Halfway down the steps, a noise stopped me. I crept into the kitchen to investigate.

"I don't know how she manages to find anything without a pantry tour guide," a familiar voice muttered. "She has these spices in completely the wrong order. As soon as I can master it, I'm going to rearrange this entire shelf."

"Good morning, Gareth." I leaned against the doorjamb, my arms folded.

He jumped out of the pantry and slammed the door, startled. "Emma! I didn't hear you come down."

"I'm glad, because then I wouldn't have learned of your evil plans for my spices."

"Sorry. You weren't meant to hear any of that," he said.

I laughed. "Why not? It's nothing you haven't said to my face."

"True." His ghostly brow furrowed. "What is it? Why do you suddenly look deranged?"

"Stars and stones," I gasped. "I think I know what happened to Ed Doyle."

Gareth drifted over to me. "He ate a spice he was allergic to and fell off the ladder in a choking fit?"

"Um, no." My head was spinning as I put the pieces of the puzzle together. "Nothing like that. I need to send a message to Markos."

"But it's so early."

"And this is urgent. Sedgwick, wake up," I yelled. "I need you." I headed into Gareth's former home office to find a quill and parchment. "I'll send a quick note and then follow up with Astrid."

I finished the note and located Sedgwick on the banister in the foyer. "Take this to Markos. It's very important."

Sedgwick groaned. *Markos again? I'll be honest. I'm starting to miss Demetrius.*

"This isn't personal," I said. "It's business."

Business? Well, in that case…

I stuffed the note into his beak before he could finish and opened the front door. "Off you go."

He glared at me as he flew out the door.

"Where are you going?" Gareth inquired, as I hurried up the stairs.

"To shower and change. I have a feeling it's going to be a busy day."

By the time I'd made myself presentable, I received a reply from Markos. Gareth placed it carefully on the dresser.

"You carried it all the way upstairs?" I asked.

He nodded proudly. "And lifted it from the front porch."

"Good job," I said. "You'll be rearranging my spices in no time."

"I might be delivering your messages, too, if your familiar decides he's too lazy to deliver the note upstairs."

"He probably went hunting," I said, scanning the note. "Markos is taking care of something at the labyrinth before he heads to the office. He wants me to meet him over there so we can decide what to do next."

"I'll hold down the fort here, as always," Gareth said, sounding mildly disappointed.

"Don't worry, Gareth," I said brightly. "You'll be tackling that pantry in no time."

The news seemed to cheer him. "Aye, I suppose I will."

"Markos, are you here?" I listened for a response or any sound of movement. I wasn't sure what he needed to take care of at the labyrinth, so I didn't know where to look. Oddly, there was no sign of his car.

I stood at the threshold of the labyrinth. Was he waiting in the place where we had our picnic? I was pretty sure I could find it. Not so sure about finding my way out, though. I decided to call him one last time.

"Markos," I yelled. "Are you okay?"

I was seized by panic. What if something happened to him? Just because he designed the labyrinth didn't mean he couldn't hurt himself in it. That possibility was enough to drive me forward. I crept along the side of the hedge and heard the vines quiver around me. Something brushed against the back of my leg and I jumped. I turned around to see the hedges shifting. If I'd known there was a chance I was going to get lost in the labyrinth, I would have brought a spool of thread or a trail of breadcrumbs. Hansel and Gretel I was not.

"I think the clearing is up ahead," I said to myself. As though the hedges heard me, they began to move again, forming a barrier around me. I whirled around, searching for the new path. There wasn't one.

"Markos?" I called again. I held my wand in front of me and desperately tried to find a way through. I couldn't turn around now—hedges blocked every possible exit.

I wondered whether I could do a spell to move one of the hedges. It was worth a try. "Time to get into the groove/magic make these hedges move." I pointed my wand at the row in front of me, but nothing happened.

"It won't work," a voice said. "Markos created the labyrinth so that spell casters couldn't manipulate it. Otherwise, it would be too easy for most residents."

Nellie.

My heart began to race.

I moved in a circle, trying to see the nymph. "Nellie, where are you? Where's Markos?"

"Markos isn't here," she said. "Your owl was kind enough to leave a note on Markos's desk alerting me to your revelation."

The office? Inwardly I groaned. Why did Sedgwick deliver the note to the office?

I smacked my forehead. "Spell's bells. I told him it was a business matter."

Nellie clucked her tongue. "Silly owl."

"Why did you lure me here?" I demanded, whirling around. I had no clue where she was.

"I thought it was time for us to have a little chat."

"A little chat or are you planning to kill me the way you killed Ed Doyle?"

Nellie chuckled from somewhere in the labyrinth. "Yes, I suppose you're right. A little chat will get us nowhere."

"So Markos didn't get the note?" At least he was home safe, even if I wasn't.

"Of course not. I'm always in the office before the boss.

How else do you think I managed to pull off my financial feats for so long without him noticing?"

"He noticed," I said. "He's been concerned about the numbers for weeks."

"Yes. He took an unexpected interest when he went over budget for the new headquarters. I had to play along and do my best to cover my tracks."

"But then Ed came along and overheard you talking to yourself about it," I said.

"I didn't realize anyone was in the building," Nellie said. "I'm usually alone at that hour. He was inspecting the top floor as I was trying to make changes to the numbers. He got an earful."

"Why did he go back to work instead of telling Markos?" I asked.

"He didn't know that I saw him," Nellie explained. "When I went downstairs to leave for the evening, I casually mentioned that Markos would be back soon if he wanted to chat about anything."

"So you kept him there."

"I waited until he took a break and then tampered with the ladder," Nellie admitted. "I saw the janitor on my way out, but I made sure he didn't see me."

"But Markos wasn't coming back to the office that night," I said.

"Of course not," she scoffed. "For a lawyer, you're pretty dim."

"Not so dim that I didn't figure out it was you," I said. "Markos has been stressed about the records. This morning I remembered that you were hard of hearing, but that you talked out loud to yourself. I finally put the pieces together."

"Which is why you're here now," Nellie said. "I couldn't let you ruin everything, could I? Things have gone too far to turn back now."

"How long have you been stealing from Markos?" I asked. I didn't really care about the answer. I only needed to stall her.

"I believe you'll find it's called embezzlement," Nellie said. "As a lawyer, I would think you'd know that."

"You seem very hung up on the fact that I'm a lawyer," I said. "Why does it bother you so much?"

"You think I dreamed of being an office manager as a young nymph? Do you think I wasn't smart enough to be more? Not all of us have been afforded the same opportunities as you, certainly not in Spellbound."

"Spellbound has lawyers," I said. "And accountants and architects and any number of so-called white collar jobs. Trust me, I didn't grow up with a silver spoon in my mouth." More like a bitter pill.

"You certainly seem to have one now. A nice house. A respected job. Friends. Males who dote on you."

The hedges around me began to grow taller. "What are you doing?"

"I've been working with Markos for years," she said. "I know every nook and cranny of this labyrinth. More importantly, I can change it."

"How do you think Markos will feel when he finds out that you not only stole from him—excuse me, embezzled from him—but that you also murdered a building inspector and the young woman he hoped to date."

"Ah, you seem to forget that the dead cannot speak," Nellie said.

"They do in my house," I said. "You won't get away with this, no matter how lucky you're feeling right now." I tried to send a mental scream to Sedgwick as I spoke, but I suspected he was too far out of range to hear me. "It's not like you can escape Spellbound. Once they realize you're the culprit, you'll have nowhere to hide."

That was one of the downsides to being a criminal in this town. Your getaway car would only get you as far as the border.

Vines slithered toward my feet and began to wrap around my legs. I tried to remain calm.

"Scratchy, aren't they?" Nellie remarked. "Some of them might be poisonous too."

"Markos would never design a feature that would hurt someone," I said.

Nellie laughed softly in the distance. "I'm a nymph, Emma. I can control any plant or shrub in this labyrinth. Markos really should do a better job of monitoring his employees. You have no idea how many pots my fingers have been in. The accounts and the labyrinth don't begin to cover it."

"Markos trusts you," I said. "That's why he doesn't monitor you closely. You've been working alongside him for years. He relies on you. Why would you use his trust against him?"

The vines squeezed my calves and the skin began to burn. Apparently, she wasn't lying about the poison.

"What's your plan? I asked. "Death by overgrowth?" I pointed my wand at the vines and said, "Read me the signs/get rid of these vines."

The vines continue to creep up to my thighs.

"I told you your witch magic won't work here," she said.

"Witch magic," I repeated softly. What if I didn't use witch magic?

I had to be careful. I couldn't let Nellie know that I had access to a different type of magic. Under the circumstances, she wouldn't hesitate to reveal my secret.

"Do me a favor and tell Markos that I really did enjoy spending time with him," I said.

"Aw, that's sweet," Nellie said, but I heard the note of

sarcasm in her voice. "I'll tell him no such thing. In fact, I might make it so that he thought you were meeting another suitor here. Your reputation would be forever tarnished in his eyes. Like that whore Eden."

"I doubt that," I said. "I've always been honest with him about the possibility of a romantic relationship with me."

"And why is that?" Nellie asked. "Is he not successful enough for you? Not attractive enough?"

"That's really none of your business," I said. "The only one who deserves that information is Markos."

The vines wrapped around my shoulders and began to squeeze my neck. If the poison didn't kill me, then the choking certainly would. I needed to dig deep and pull from that special place inside me where the sorceress magic lived. I had only tapped into it once before, to save my life during my escape from Felix, the angry wizard.

I tried to relax my shoulders and focus inward. Even though sorcery was allegedly steeped in darkness, I'd managed to tap into a positive place and draw strength from that. It was worth another try.

I breathed in my mother's scent, remembering the feel of her arms around me. No one in the world gave hugs like my mother. Then I focused my will on the vines and said in my firmest voice, "Release."

The vines snapped and dropped to the ground. The cuts on my arms continued to burn. There was likely poison coursing through my veins. I needed to get out of here and get help.

"You're awfully quiet in there," Nellie said. "Are you dead yet?"

"I'm sorry to disappoint you," I said. My best bet was to retrace my steps back to the car. The problem was that I had no idea where Nellie was hiding.

I focused my will on the hedges behind me. "Move," I

commanded. The hedges shifted in response and I began to run, thrashing as vines reached out to grab me.

"How are you doing this?" Nellie cried. "You're not a nymph."

I saw her in the clearing as I fell to the ground. The poison was working its way through my system, and I realized I was about to lose consciousness. I tried to crawl across the silky grass, but my legs and arms gave out and I slid into darkness.

CHAPTER 19

MY MOUTH TASTED like a container of cotton and my throat burned. I opened my eyes to see Markos hovering next to me. "What…Where am I?"

"In your room," he replied. "I carried you here after I found you unconscious at the labyrinth. Boyd's already been here to administer the antidote to the poison."

"And I kept an eye on Markos," Gareth said from his place in the corner. "Made sure he didn't try anything funny."

I resisted the urge to smile. Gareth knew perfectly well that Markos wasn't that kind of minotaur.

"How do you feel?" Markos asked, offering me a glass of water. I drank greedily.

"My body hurts," I said, and the events of the morning came rushing back to me. "Did you catch Nellie?"

Markos nodded gravely. "Unfortunately, she didn't make it out of the labyrinth alive. When she saw me coming, she tried to run away. She didn't realize I was more focused on helping you. I found her later tangled in poisonous vines, but it was too late."

"She's a nymph, though," I said. "Why didn't she untangle herself?"

"The vines were a special variety called the Goose's Noose. The more she tried to untangle herself, the tighter the vines got."

She was probably so desperate to escape Markos that she wasn't thinking clearly.

Markos pressed his fingers to his temples. "I don't even know how they got there. I don't use poisonous plants in my designs."

"I'm afraid you actually do." I told him what Nellie said about her involvement. "I'm sorry."

"Me too," Markos said. "What a mess."

"How did you know to find us there?" I asked.

"Your owl," he said, nodding toward Sedgwick feigning sleep on his perch. "He came to the office and seemed to be expecting something."

"A reply," I said. "He left you a note and came back to see if you had a response."

Markos shrugged. "I didn't know what he wanted because there was no note, but he became agitated and flew around the office in a frenzy. He's the one who saw your car parked at the labyrinth."

"The view from your office," I said quietly.

He smirked. "And here I thought it was nice to have bragging rights. Turns out it comes in handy, too."

I squeezed his arm. "Thank you for rescuing me."

Markos shook his head. "You got yourself out of there. I only carried you home so Boyd could deal with the poison." He turned to face the wall, his expression clouding over. "Between Eden and Nellie, I'm beginning to think I should develop trust issues."

I reached over to cover his hand with mine. "Please don't,

Markos. The world is a much better place when we trust each other."

"Are you up for more visitors?" Markos asked. "Sheriff Astrid was around earlier. She said to send Sedgwick when you were able to talk."

From his nearby perch, Sedgwick groaned. *Now I'm taking orders from the bull and the crazy blonde? I don't think so.*

You're taking orders from me, I said. *Deal with it.*

I noticed a cup of tea on the bedside table. "Oh, perfect. Thank you, Markos."

He glanced at the cup. "That wasn't me. I only brought the water."

Gareth wiggled his fingers from his place in the corner and my face lit up.

"You made me tea?" I couldn't hide my excitement.

"I assume you're talking to Gareth and not the spider in the corner," Markos said.

Gareth whipped around. "There's a spider?"

I laughed. "This is the best news I've had in a long time."

"Don't get used to it, missy," Gareth said. "I'm not taking on the role of your butler."

"But you said you wanted to be useful," I reminded him.

"You might also want to send Sedgwick over to the coven," Markos said. "Your friends were pestering Boyd for an update."

"Okay, thanks." I hesitated, afraid to ask my next question. "Anyone else?"

Markos gave me a sorrowful look. "No, Emma. I'm sorry."

"Word probably hasn't gotten around yet," Gareth offered.

In Spellbound? Not likely.

I sat up in bed and tried to stay positive. I was alive and well and surrounded by friends who cared about me. That was enough. It had to be.

Markos positioned himself on the edge of the bed. "Emma, I apologize for getting you into this mess with Nellie. If it wasn't for me, this whole thing never would've happened."

"Don't be silly," I said. "It's not your fault. Nellie took advantage of your kindness."

He ran his hands through his thick hair. "I don't mean to be difficult, especially not when you're still recovering, but do you think there's any chance your feelings for me might change? I don't want to get my hopes up, not after waiting so long to meet someone special."

"I understand, Markos," I said. "The truth is, as long as I have any hope of bringing Daniel back to reality, I can't consider starting a relationship with anyone else. My heart wouldn't be in it and that's not fair to you or me."

His expression softened. "That's what I thought you'd say." He hesitated. "What do you mean about bringing Daniel back to reality?"

I wasn't ready to share my Obsession potion theory with too many people. Word could reach Elsa before I implemented my plan and I couldn't risk the blowback.

"Nothing," I said quickly. "He hasn't been acting like himself since he got engaged. That's all."

"I hope things work out for you, Emma. I really do. You deserve to be happy."

I patted his hand. "We all do, Markos."

I heard the thundering footsteps downstairs and knew that the remedial witches had arrived.

"Emma," they shouted.

"It's like a stampede," Markos observed, as the girls rushed into the room.

"I'm fine," I said. "No need to panic."

"Spell's bells," Begonia said. "Stop scaring us with your near death experiences."

"It would be my pleasure," I said wryly.

Markos rubbed his hands on his thighs. "That's my cue to get out of your hair."

"Thanks, Markos," I said. "For everything. We'll see each other again soon, right?"

"I hope so."

"I'll walk him out," Gareth said, following him through the doorway.

"You just want to stare at his butt," I accused, and Gareth turned back to wiggle his eyebrows.

"It is a nice butt," Begonia said, craning her neck to catch a glimpse before Markos disappeared from view.

"We're so glad you're okay," Sophie said, throwing herself on the bed beside me.

"Thanks," I said. "Me too. I guess I missed class."

"Don't worry about it," Laurel said. "Ginger taught today and you know how relaxed she is."

"And now we can focus on our extracurricular spell," Millie said. "That is, if you feel up to it."

"At least give her a few hours to recuperate first," Sophie said.

I took a sip of my tea. "I'll be ready this afternoon. Believe me, nobody wants this spell to work more than I do." The closer I was to invisibility, the closer I was to exposing Elsa's deception and freeing Daniel.

"You don't have to go to the office?" Begonia asked.

I broke into a wide smile. "Not today. My schedule is clear." And so was the path ahead. I knew exactly what I had to do and how to do it. The thought gave me considerable comfort.

"You seem awfully happy for a witch who was close to death this morning," Sophie said.

I stretched my arms above my head, ready to face the day. "I am happy, Sophie. Things are going to turn around for me soon. I feel it in my bones."

"I think the poison may have gone to her brain," Millie said.

"You'll see, Millie," I said. "With your help, we're going to thwart Elsa's plan and stop the wedding."

"And Emma will finally get her HEA," Begonia said, clapping her hands.

"Happily Ever After," I whispered to myself.

I certainly wouldn't object to that.

* * *

Thank you for reading **_Better Than Hex_**! If you enjoyed it, please help other readers find this book ~

1. Write a review and post it on Amazon.

2. Sign up for my new releases via e-mail here http://eepurl.com/ctYNzf or like me on Facebook so you can find out about the next book before it's even available.

3. Look out for **_Cast Away_**, the sixth book in the series!

Made in the USA
Monee, IL
26 February 2022

91928073R10111